DAUGHTER OF HADES

ENTANGLED

BOOK THREE

FoxTales Press

DANI HOOTS

Entangled
Daughter of Hades, #3
© 2020 FoxTales Press
Content and line edits by Justin Boyer
Cover Design Copyright © 2019 by Biserka Designs
Formatting by Dani Hoots
All rights reserved.

ISBN for Paperback: 978-1-942023-69-2

ISBN for Hardcover: 978-1-942023-70-8

Chapter 1

CHRYS

Today marked my last day in the Underworld, as there were two weeks left before the autumn equinox. There had to be a way out of the marriage, and Huntley would find the means. Although I had the strength to free myself, I understood that my father would pay the price for my rebellion. Zeus might hurt my mother, father, or maybe even Huntley if I tried to escape. I wouldn't let that happen. No, I accepted my fate unless Huntley and the others found a loophole. He was a human, but he was smart and would go to the ends of the Earth to help me.

I enjoyed the summer months learning from my father, even if Hermes showed up whenever he wanted. Hermes annoyed Hades less, but still got on Hades' nerves at least once a day. I stayed out of their feud, once I learned their argument was centuries in the making. Their interactions delighted me, though.

Father put together a big dinner tonight. The dinner seemed odd to hold as the whole situation wasn't something to celebrate, even if it was for a wedding. My heart felt as if it skipped a beat every time I thought about leaving this place. I wanted more than anything to get out of this mess, but it was my fault this was all going on—I should have just stayed in the Underworld and never ventured to the mortal realm. Father almost died because of my mistake, and now I had to face the consequences.

During the last few months, I grew fond of Hermes and considered him an excellent friend, even if he was working for Zeus. I didn't have many friends to begin with, as I couldn't interact with other gods in fear they would report back to Zeus. The only friends I had were Huntley, Maka, and AJ, but AJ didn't consider me a friend. He just used me to get out of the Underworld. He lied to me for centuries, starving himself and acting like he cared for me.

The betrayal still burned, and I didn't think I could ever forgive him. It seemed like most gods were like that though—not possessing the ability to forgive. I dreamt about getting my revenge on him someday, but decided he wasn't worth the effort. If I crossed paths with him one day, however, I doubted I could hold back my wrath.

I couldn't wait for that day.

Hermes and I were outside on the balcony, watching the shimmer of Oceana glisten from the sunlight in the mortal realm, and the rainfall of souls into Tartarus. I could even see Charon in the distance, guiding the souls that Hades would judge himself. I wondered how many of the souls that went to Tartarus even believed that it existed. I had heard it all while judging with my father: I didn't know; I made a mistake; I was just a human; there were no signs. Any excuse they came up with was meaningless. They just said it to save their skin, or soul, not because they felt guilt. They should realize the God of the Underworld could see through their lies and into their souls. I guess if they were that smart, they wouldn't be on their way to Tartarus.

It felt as if Hermes was looking over at me instead of out to the distance, so I peeked over at him. I was right; he was staring right at me with his aquamarine eyes.

"What?" I asked.

He laughed and shook his head. "You and your father are a lot alike. Although, I think you are kinder than he is."

I didn't think I was like my father at all—he was benevolent, a hard worker, but stern in a caring way. "No, he's a lot stronger than I am. He is a bold leader of this world and I can't even look at my future without trembling."

"I think that is where you are wrong. You are stronger than you realize. And besides, between you and me, he's always fearful. But that makes people strong," Hermes explained.

"What do you mean?"

"If you had nothing be afraid of—if you felt no pain—then what is there to be brave about? No, the ones who struggle the most are the strongest because they keep on going even against all odds."

I liked how Hermes could be sarcastic and troublesome one moment and compassionate and caring the next. Although I don't think I had ever seen him be compassionate when my father was around. I guess he only did that for me.

"Thank you, Hermes, I needed to hear that."

"My pleasure. Now we better not keep your

father waiting any longer."

I chuckled. "That's the first time I've heard you say that."

"Well, tonight is different. I don't want to push any of his buttons. Not for a while, at least."

I knew what he meant by that. I let out a sigh and followed him back into the dark-stoned castle. I would miss this place, as I doubted Zeus' home was a gothic-style castle like something out of Dracula. Although my mother always hated how brooding it felt, I loved it. I would still get to be home most of the year, when my mother was in the mortal realm. I made sure that was part of the deal as Zeus had forced the same when my father married. It was only three months of the year. That wouldn't be that awful, right?

As we stepped inside, Cerberus came running into the hallway, his three heads bouncing up and down. I didn't even need to kneel for him to lick my face. I would miss him while I was away, especially since I would know my mother would shrug him off and ignore him for the time she was here. She always seemed to loathe him, even though he was her pet. At least father would be here to spoil Cerberus as much as he could.

"That dog likes you," Hermes commented as I

rubbed Cerberus' belly.

Cerberus turned and growled at him. I laughed. "He likes me, yes, but I thought by now he would have warmed up to you. I guess not."

"Yeah, well, I think your father has trained him to hate me."

"Fair enough. I think I might have seen him whispering things in Cerberus' ear about you. If I were you, I wouldn't come down here unless I'm around just to be safe."

Hermes monitored Cerberus, who was still glaring at him. "I'll keep that in mind."

We headed down towards the dining room where a feast was waiting. I was curious what my father had prepared for the night. I wasn't even sure who would be there, especially since I didn't have that many people close to me.

Opening the door to the dining hall, Hermes ushered me inside. I gasped in astonishment at all the food that lined the table. It was every kind of food I had ever loved, including memorable dishes I had eaten when I visited London—scones and pots of tea. How he found out about me loving it, I had no idea. There also my favorite German dish käsespätzle, crème brûlée, roasted veggies with herbs, and Black Forest cake.

My eyes were so glued to the food that it took a second to see the other people gathered around the table. Maka, the three stooges, Charon, Nyx, whom I hadn't seen in forever, and Hekate They were all here to see me off, even though I rarely saw them and leaving for Olympus would not change the amount of time I would see them. But father must have asked them to come and although I knew they would never go against a request of his, they would have come either way to see me off. I smiled and gave Maka a brief nod to tell her thank you. I couldn't remember the last time she was in the palace like this. She was typically far too busy, so it surprised me to see her on this side of the Underworld. They were all busy, to be honest, but they put their lives on hold for this last dinner before seeing me off.

Hermes pulled out the chair for me, and I took a seat. Everyone was so quiet that it was a little awkward. I didn't know what to break the silence. I feared that if I opened my mouth, I would weep. I glanced over at my father who must have understood. He tapped his wine glass to call attention for a speech.

"Everyone, help yourself."

With that, everyone loaded their plates with the

food father had prepared. Words and laughter filled the room as the gods and goddesses filled in each other on all the adventures they had since the last time they had seen one another other. From some conversations, it was clear some of these gods hadn't seen each other for centuries. Maka, who sat across from me, sipped on tea that I questioned whether it was a type she had bought, or if my dad had made a special brew just for her.

"Don't worry, child, this is not the end. You are still a part of the Underworld, no matter where you go." She glanced over at Hades. "Just like your father."

"I know, it's just going to be hard to adjust is all. Everything of mine is here, and the times I'm gone I will miss the shimmer of Oceana. I have never even been to Olympus, I don't know what to expect."

"It's a beautiful place," Hermes chimed in. "It is filled with gold and clouds, and everything seems to be glowing."

Father interrupted. "Including people's egos. The land may be beautiful, my flower, but the people aren't. Everyone up there is ready to stab each other in the back, so be careful to guard yourself as I won't be there to keep you safe."

Maka placed her hand on his shoulder. "Don't

worry, Hades, she will be fine. She is strong, remember? She went up against Poseidon himself. I doubt anyone will cause her any trouble."

"Man I wish I got to see that," Hermes commented. "There aren't many who can take him down. I would have sold tickets to all the other gods to watch and made an enormous bowl of popcorn."

I saw the side of father's mouth twitch, as if he would smile, but he didn't let anyone see he found it amusing.

"I'm still not sure how I did that, and also those powers are the reason…" I trailed off, not wanting to bring up the marriage with father there. It was still hard for him to talk about.

"So you will be with Persephone for the next two weeks, right?" Maka asked. "You will see what it is like for gods on the other side through her lens. I think that will be an interesting experience for both of you."

I shrugged, not wanting to talk about mother to her. I still wasn't happy with the way things ended with her and I didn't want to admit it. I was also not sure if spending two weeks with her would be fun or awful. If history repeated itself, which it did, it would be the worst experience of my life. But then I wouldn't ever have to see her again, at least not if I didn't want to. She would be in the Underworld while I lived in Olympus, and I would be in the Underworld while she lived in the mortal realm. It was a win-win for where our relationship was at the moment.

"And Demeter," Hermes added. "You have never met your grandmother, have you?"

I shook my head. "No, I have not."

Father mumbled under his breath so I only could hear. "Ugly old cow, if you ask me."

I chuckled, and we gave each other a smile. I didn't know what to expect with Demeter, and could only imagine her to be like my mother, but worse.

"What did I miss?" Maka asked.

I shook my head. "Nothing. Don't worry about it."

"Probably something about Demeter, if I'm not wrong." Hermes took a bite of his steak. "Hades has never gotten along with her. Actually he doesn't get along with anyone who isn't in the Underworld."

"That's because no one down here is a backstabbing liar."

Hades and Hermes stared at each other while Maka and I laughed. I didn't want tonight to end.

Chapter 2

HUNTLEY

Two weeks remained until the Autumn Equinox—the day Chrys was supposed to marry Zeus. I didn't like how close we were to the official day, but we had to wait until she was in Olympus. It was the only way to get to her, as no god wanted to journey down to the Underworld in fear of never returning. Once Chrys was in Olympus, Persephone could set everything up, help us get to her once we sneaked in, and then Prometheus would use the box to save her.

The box that Hades had given me to give to Prometheus was still a mystery to me. I wanted to know what was in it, and wanted to quote Brad Pitt in the movie *Se7en*, but stayed on the safe side and not foolishly open a box a god gave me. I had heard the tale of Pandora's box, and I would not make that same mistake. I would find out when I needed to, and I was fine with that.

According to Prometheus, whatever the contents in the box were, they would guarantee that Chrys couldn't marry Zeus. He said that it would make it so him and Chrys were already married, and even though that wasn't true, they would have to fake it for some time. I did not like this part of the plan, as I didn't want Chrys marrying anyone she didn't want to, and because I wanted to be with her. Prometheus ensured me they wouldn't actually be married and that she and I could live freely in the Underworld, where Zeus wouldn't see. Although I knew I could trust Prometheus, as he had done nothing but help me and Chrys, I still didn't like this plan.

But it was our only shot.

However, we had to wait until Chrys was in Olympus, which made me worry even more. If, for some reason, it didn't work, that meant we had to scramble for a backup plan. We had been trying to come up with one, but to my knowledge, and to the other's, there was no other way without facing Zeus, and possibly getting killed, or worse.

So that left me waiting—still stuck in a flat in the

middle of London that Pothos owned. It was him, Prometheus, Melinoe, and I all staying at the flat. Luckily it was a rather large flat, and a lot larger than the trailer I grew up in. Although Mel hung all over Prometheus all the time, it was still much, much more tolerable than that trailer, as now I didn't have anyone screaming at me, hitting me, telling me I was worthless…

I mean, they called me human in a derogatory manner, but after seeing what they were capable of, I didn't protest. Humans were nothing compared to gods, but I was showing I could hold my own.

Persephone and her sirens were at the flat, often helping with the plan, but they had their own place somewhere in Kensington. I thought about asking Persephone if I could stay with her, as sometimes Mel and Prometheus got on my nerves, but I decided against it. Anytime she wasn't around, and the sirens of hers were, I felt like they were plotting my demise. If I was all alone in my room, asleep, I wasn't sure if they would come in and kill me or not.

So I took my chances with Mel instead, but she too was scary. She was the goddess of ghosts. When she was sleeping, she tended to conjure up some scary things. Luckily, Prometheus could wake her before anything disastrous happened. She loved him and he, for some bizarre reason, didn't mind. They spent more time in their room than I had ever seen from any other couple. I still didn't quite understand what she saw in him, especially since when they were out of the bedroom, he just treated her as if she were some accessory, while she draped herself all over him. Half the time she said something to him, he didn't reply. Yet she still was as infatuated as ever with him.

It was like high school all over again.

The eight of us, including Persephone and the sirens, sat around the dining table Pothos had, which was really made for six, but we made it work. Normally he didn't make it a habit to eat dinner together like this, but since this was the night before Persephone would take Chrys to Olympus, we figured it would be better to sit down and talk everything out. We ordered Chinese food, believe it or not, as none of the gods cared to cook. The restaurant down the street was rather tasty, though, so I never complained. And I didn't have to pay for it.

My favorite was the orange chicken, and I was quick to grab it each time. However, this time, one siren grabbed it before me and laughed in triumph.

"What will the little human do, now that I have his favorite food?" Peisinoe, or Peisy, laughed.

"Peisy," Persephone sighed. "Give him his food back."

Peisy frowned and handed me the orange chicken. I gulped, hoping she didn't somehow curse it. You never knew with these people, I swore. I felt minuscule around them, but they always included me in everything at least. They pointed out often that I was weaker than them, but I didn't feel like an outsider anymore. It was a strange feeling that I didn't know how to handle. All my life I felt as if I was an outsider, never having a place where I really belonged. It wasn't until I met Chrys that I found someone who understood me and felt cared for. Now I didn't feel like the outcast, having this group and everything. That was why I felt I owed Chrys everything and would do anything I could to give her the happiness she deserved.

Dumping out some orange chicken on my plate, I passed it down and grabbed some fried rice and spicy pork. Not much was said as everyone filled their plates. Any moment now, though, Prometheus would probably say a comment that would piss off the sirens and there would be a lot of hissing as their faces became scary water beasts that freaked me out every time. When they were in their human form, they were gorgeous. They each had fiery red hair, light skin and freckles, and green eyes, but the moment they turned into their other form, their teeth became sharp, shark teeth, their skin turned greenish-blue, and their eyes went pitch black. It was creepy as fuck.

Luckily, I stayed on their good side by keeping my mouth shut, or at least what I considered being their good side. They didn't threaten me out loud. Many teachers, and parents, and any adult really, would have been surprised by my quietness around them. They did everything to shut me up when I was first alive. I never did. At least not until I overdosed. Even today, I wondered how many of them were relieved I was gone.

But that was a past life, and today was a different me. But man, it took everything I had not to have some good comebacks for these three. They were annoying some days, but they were definitely more frightening than they were annoying. So kept my mouth shut.

All the food was poured out on the plates and still no one said a word. The sounds of everyone's forks or chopsticks hitting the plates seemed even louder than normal. I wasn't used to this much silence and bounced my leg enough where I could tell I was shaking the table. Pothos glared at me and I stopped. I couldn't help it, there was too much restless energy inside of me and I had to move.

Persephone placed her hand on my knee. "It's all right, Huntley, things will go as planned. I don't doubt it for a second."

I nodded and picked at my food with my fork. I always picked out all the peas in the fried rice because I thought they had a weird consistency. I had five in a clump now.

"Hey Persephone, does it bug you that Huntley picks at his vegetables, since, well, you know, you are the goddess of spring and vegetation and all that?" Prometheus snickered from the other end of the table.

I shot him a look. "I just don't like how they are cooked; it has nothing to do with whom made them."

"Huntley can like whatever he wants, Prometheus. It's not like I created them, I just make sure they flourish. Now shut up before I wipe that grin off your face, okay?" Persephone stared at Prometheus. He chuckled a little, then went back to his food.

Man, I loved having dinner with these people. It

was so much fun.

"He has a point," Aglaope, also known as Aggie, commented. "This measly human should just eat everything and be thankful to you for the food he can eat. Remember, in the old days, when people weren't picky about their food? How each one of them had to work hard in the fields to survive? Now they can just go down to the supermarket and buy whatever they want. Hell, they can even have it delivered already cooked. These humans are spoiled."

Persephone said nothing, but just gave Aggie a look. She quickly stopped talking and went back to her dinner. It was fun to see Persephone order people around like she did, even if she wasn't always the best mom to Chrys. It seemed like she was trying to make up for that, though, by being supportive now and helping stop this wedding. I wondered if she felt a teensy-bit responsible, since it was because of her that Chrys ran off into the mortal realm. But I would not bring that up… again.

Rain hit the windows, causing a rather dreary September day, which seemed to be the norm. I lived in Philadelphia where it rained more, but it felt drearier here. I wasn't sure if it was because it hardly snowed in London. Either way, I found myself sick of the rain, and wished we moved some place warmer, like Crete or something.

Pothos was first to finish and pushed his plate forward. "Well, that was a pleasant dinner. I swear they become better cooks every time. As for Huntley, not so much."

"Hey! At least I try! You never try to cook and just laze around."

Pothos shrugged. "What can I say, I'm used to being served."

I grabbed a plastic spoon and threw it at him. It bounced off his laughing face. "Oh Huntley, you are always so quick to start a fight. I will miss you when all of this is over."

Everyone went silent, as we all realized we had never discussed what would happen when all of this was over. My plan, of course, was to go back to the Underworld with Chrys, since that was where I was supposed to be, but I didn't think about how this normal life would be no more. Even though they were all a pain in my ass, I considered them all to be my friends. I came to cherish these past few months, and understood how much they wanted to help Chrys, or at least not let Zeus have his way. I would get to see them again, wouldn't I?

I realized for a moment that the likelihood of

seeing them all again was slim to none. No one went to visit the Underworld, and as I learned before, those who were in the Underworld didn't exactly get to come up topside like this. How could I be so stupid to not realize that?

"It's been great, you know?" I whispered. "I am thankful that all of you are trying to help Chrys and have included me."

Persephone smiled and placed her hand on my back.

Pothos threw the plastic spoon back at me. "You idiot, don't get sappy. We are gods, we will see each other again. Might not be for a long while, but we will. Besides, you still have some time with us. You aren't out of this yet."

"We still have to make it to Olympus, which will be an adventure in its own right. And not get caught. This is definitely not over, so don't be saying your goodbyes yet," Prometheus added.

That was true. We still had two weeks before the wedding, and I still wasn't sure what would happen once we launched our plan to convince Zeus that Chrys had already been married to Prometheus. Maybe Chrys and I could live in the mortal realm during that time, which would be cool to travel everywhere together.

But if she was pretending to be married to Prometheus, could I still see her?

The plan was to go back to the Underworld, but what did that mean for Prometheus? Would she have to leave the Underworld every few months and stay with Prometheus? I had so many questions that I knew there wouldn't be an answer to until all of this was over with. We just had to save her. We had to.

Or I would die trying.

Chapter 3

CHRYS

Packing sucked.

I never had to pack before, other than to go to Maka's, but that was usually only for a night or two. This was different as I had to pack for three months, plus the wedding. Granted, Zeus would probably give me anything I needed, but some things just needed to be brought along in order to make it feel like home.

There was no way Olympus would ever feel like home. Even if I blacked out the windows and closed my eyes. Nowhere was as nice as the Underworld, I learned that the hard way, as I wanted to see how nice the mortal world was compared to here. It sucked, and I wished I never had stepped foot on it.

Mainly because I wouldn't have been in this mess if I just had stay put.

I blamed A.J. and my mother often, but I knew that the choice had been ultimately mine. It didn't change the fact that they had definitely pushed me into making the bad choice, but I tried to let it go.

And I tried not to think about the fact my mother was the one picking me up from here and taking me to Olympus.

I stuffed my bag with my stuffed giraffe, some underwear, and some outfits that Huntley liked the best. There wasn't a day that went by that I didn't miss him. He was on Earth, probably trying to do the impossible. No, I knew he was trying to do the impossible as he had made his way to the Underworld to talk to my father about finding a way out of this. I tried to ask my father about the details, but he didn't want to put me in danger in case Hermes or Zeus started questioning things. It made sense, but I hated being out of the loop.

So I was stuck, which bugged me even more. I was a goddess—I shouldn't feel helpless. However, my every movement was watched by Hermes so I couldn't do anything to get out of this marriage with him here. Hermes would just report it quickly to Zeus. So I had to see what the others came up with, and if that didn't work, I would figure something out in Olympus.

If all else failed, I could just…

I shook my head. No, I could not use my powers the way I wanted to. I wasn't strong enough to take down Zeus or anyone like that. He would just kill me in an instant, and then father would be extremely upset. I couldn't do that to him. Not again.

"You know, you really don't even need to pack anything, Olympus has everything you have ever needed and more," Hermes said from the corner he was leaning in.

I jumped a little, deep in thought, and forgetting he was in my room. Normally he didn't come into my room, as it was my little sanctuary, but since we were about to leave, he stayed near in case I tried to make any last escape.

I sighed. "You don't understand, these things mean a lot to me."

"Including those pink undies? I mean they are cute, but I don't see the emotional connection…"

I threw my pillow at him as hard as I could. I heard him grunt as it hit him in the stomach.

"I just want to make sure I'm prepared for anything. And I don't want to rely on others to give me everything. Besides, I like the way these fit, and I'm not sure what kind of underwear they have in Olympus, probably just a piece of string knowing you all."

Hermes laughed. "You aren't wrong. Just hurry it up a little, we are leaving within an hour."

"Yeah, I know. I waited until last minute because I didn't want to do this."

"You mean you didn't want to leave."

I nodded. I really, really didn't want to leave. I wished I had stayed in the Underworld like I was supposed to and not gotten myself into this mess. If I had just done what I was told…

Tears fell down my check as I put away the rest of my clothes in the luggage bag.

Hermes moved towards me and placed his hand on my shoulder. "It's okay. Everything will be fine. It's just three months. You will be back here before you know it."

I smiled a little. "Thanks. I hope so."

"And your father will be there on the wedding day, so you have nothing to worry about. He wouldn't let you do this on your own, all right? You are his only daughter, a genuine miracle. No one thought it was possible."

"Which is why he hid me—because the daughter

of death would be the one who would make the Gods of Olympus be no more."

"Yeah, because of that. No pressure."

I rolled my eyes. It was a prophecy that I now finally understood. Since I could control both life and death, the gods feared me. I could kill any of them with my power, something that was normally not easily done, and then I could bring them or anyone else back to life. I did it to Poseidon repeatedly, and that was a beacon to everyone that I existed. If I had just never used my powers, none of this would have happened.

Then again, I would be at the bottom of the ocean floor if it weren't for my powers.

Everything that had happened in London felt like it was only yesterday. I couldn't believe that it had been months ago—that it had been months since I had last seen Huntley. Well, until he snuck into my room and we…

I tried to hide my blushing from Hermes, as he would make a comment and wonder what I was thinking about. No, I didn't want him to know. It was bad enough that father had found out—not to mention I wasn't supposed to talk to Huntley ever again, by order of Zeus.

Father never made a comment about it, which I

was thankful for. I just hoped that Huntley was still alive after father went to talk to him. I doubted father would have killed him that moment, and besides, we were in the Underworld. I would have known if he had died.

Unless father was mad enough to send him to Tartarus…

I didn't believe that was possible, as father mentioned he would figure out a way out of this, when Hermes let us be alone the few times that he did. I knew my father was planning something with Huntley, but wouldn't give me any more details than that. I was just glad for once they were working together, and that he was growing fond of him, or at least using him to help me. Either way, he didn't kill Huntley.

I glanced around for anything else that I thought I might need while I was away. Opening up a drawer, I found the last bag of pomegranate seed that Huntley used to steal. I had forgotten about it and didn't think there were any left. I bit my lip, wondering how I could sneak some with me to Olympus. Perhaps they would have something as equally great in Olympus, like some enchanted apple or something. I had heard Dionysius made some fabulous wine. At least there was that.

Hermes glanced around at my band posters. "You have some weird music tastes. I'm surprised your father lets you listen to such trash."

He was looking at the Oomph! poster I had. "I'll have you know, Huntley introduced me to those bands and I like them a lot."

"Of course he did. He seems like the metal type."

"Metal is just poetry told with extreme emotions," I said. "At least, that was how Huntley put it."

"Poetry is already full of extreme emotions. Metal is just angry yelling about something. No, I prefer classic rock myself."

"You mean angstly crying about one girl or another?"

"Exactly."

I shook my head as I packed some of my hoodies. "What is Olympus like?" I asked Hermes as I added a few more black shirts. For some reason I figured there wouldn't be much black clothing available in Olympus.

He leaned back. "Well, I can tell you now you will stand out with all that black clothing."

I knew it. "I don't care, I enjoy wearing it."

"You are definitely your father's daughter. Anyway, it is like living in a perfect vacation getaway, with an endless coast, sunshine, very little clouds, and perfect homes that look like something out of Greece, since we taught them architecture."

"Sounds perfect. Other than all the gods and Zeus and whatnot."

Hermes shrugged. "Can't always be perfect. But you will get to know people and learn who to avoid. Like Apollo. You should avoid Apollo."

"Why?" I asked. No one had really talked about him before, but I knew he was the god of the sun, and much more.

"He's just… into some weird stuff. I think it would be best for you just to stay away."

"Aren't all the gods all into some weird shit?"

He laughed. "Yeah, I suppose they are. You have little to fear, though, as you will be the wife of Zeus. No one dares to cross him."

"I just have to worry about Zeus then."

"Uh… well… And Hera. But don't be too worried about her, I'm sure she has calmed down in these past few months. I'll be around so don't worry about it."

I was worrying about it. There were so many gods I wasn't sure what to worry about anymore. They all had different powers, just like me. I, however, was just a little more powerful than most. Except I wasn't supposed to use my powers.

This would go swimmingly.

I heard a knock on my door and turned to find my father standing in the doorway. He looked like he hadn't slept all night, which was saying a lot since he was a god and didn't need sleep.

"Can I have a moment alone with my daughter?" Hades asked.

Hermes hesitated for a moment, then nodded. He probably didn't want to get any more on father's bad side and understood we needed to have time alone before all this happened. He walked out of my room and closed the door. Father walked over to my bed and sat down, patting the comforter for me to sit next to him. I put away the rest of my underwear and did just as he asked. We were both quiet for a moment, waiting for someone to say something, but not wanting to face the inevitable discussion that we were about to have.

Both of us turned to each other, opening our mouths to say something. I chuckled a little.

"You first," he said.

I wrapped my arms around him. "I'm sorry, father. I'm sorry everything ended up like this because of me. I wish I could change what happened, but I…" the last few words were barely recognizable as tears and snot came running down my face, and onto father's suit.

He held me close. "Shhhh, it's okay. You will be okay. I'm not mad at you, you are my precious flower. Nothing you do will ever change that. I just wish I could help you, but I can't. I feel helpless, which is saying a lot considering I'm the oldest of all the gods of Olympus."

I laughed a little. It was strange hearing him say that he was helpless, as he was one of the strongest men I knew. It felt comforting that he still loved me, after all that had happened. He had been mad in the beginning, but understood that he couldn't be angry at something that wasn't changeable. Hermes may have helped out in that conversation, which I was thankful for. I was surprised he wasn't more thankful to Hermes for bringing us back together, but I guess centuries of other problems couldn't be fixed in a couple of months. No, I suspected father would ever trust any of the other gods, especially after all this.

He pulled back and wiped away my tears with his thumb. "Now, I have something for you."

Father pulled out a small round piece of wood from his pocket. It was intricately designed, and he opened it up to reveal a music box. It played a sweet tune that I had never heard before.

I carefully grabbed it and studied it closer. "This is beautiful. Where did you get it?"

"I had one of my men go fetch it from a small town in Russia. There is a family famous for generations for making them. I got one of the first ones the family ever made for your mother a couple of centuries ago."

I could have done without the last part, but I loved the gift either way. I studied the dark wood framework, with the floral designs that had been etched into it—chrysanthemums, of course. There was plenty of room to put some jewelry in the box's interior, and maybe even some notes.

Or even some pomegranates.

Once he left the room, I would sneak the pomegranates into here before Hermes got back. It was perfect. It wasn't like Hermes would check it, as it was just an innocent music box.

"I love it. I will listen to it every day when I get up and when I go to bed." I gave him a hug. "I'll always cherish it."

He wrapped his arms around me even tighter. "I'm doing everything I can, okay?" He whispered in my ear. "But if for some reason I fail, I want you to know, it's okay to kill him."

I laughed a little, knowing he was being serious.

He wanted to kill Zeus himself, but knew he wasn't strong enough, as Zeus was the god of all gods.

"I don't think that would be a good idea, but if it comes down to it, I will make you proud."

He let out a brief chuckle. "That's my girl."

We sat there, silent again, not wanting to leave each other's embrace. I knew I would see him again in two weeks, but it wouldn't be the same—I wouldn't be able to talk to him like I always did, nor be able to see him smile and be held like this. No, it would be a formal event where I would have to maintain a smile and hold back all my tears.

"Well, you should finish up your packing. I will send Hermes back in after I have a talk with him. I want to make sure he understands that I don't want anything to happen to my daughter."

I smiled. "Thank you."

I watched as father left me and I quickly put the pomegranates in the music box. At least I had something to pass the time with in Olympus.

Chapter 4

HUNTLEY

"You understand the plan?" Persephone asked one more time. All eight of us sat in the living room area, discussing the last part of the plan. I sat on the floor, crisscrossed, as there wasn't enough sofa space for me to sit, not to mention I wanted more room to sway back and forth. I had to get my energy out somehow.

I leaned back, rubbed my temples with my free hand. "I thought you were the one who would get us into Olympus. That was the whole reason we had been waiting all this time."

She shook her head. "No, the reason you had been waiting all this time was because we needed Chrys in Olympus so it was easier to get to her, and to show Zeus that her and Prometheus are together. I do not have the authority nor the capacity to bring anyone into Olympus. That is why you all will need to find Aphrodite."

I rubbed my forehead some more, not able to believe this was happening. "And where the hell is Aphrodite?"

Thelia answered, tossing her wavy red hair to the side. "Last I heard, she was in Paris. Maybe Milan? Pretty sure it was Paris."

Great, she was in another country. This was never easy. "I don't have a passport as I'm not actually alive."

Persephone snapped her fingers, and a passport appeared. "You forget, Huntley, we are gods."

I took a deep breath. "If you could do that, then why don't you snap Chrys here and we hide?"

Persephone gave me a look. "You know if that was possible we would have already done it. No, we have to be careful when treading these waters, Huntley. Zeus is not a god you want to piss off."

Prometheus commented. "That is quite a fact."

They had a point, but even so it seemed like more and more gods wanted to help us. All of them were sick of Zeus and wanted his reign to end. Would it be hard to convince them that Chrys could destroy him? And then if we had enough people on our side, Chrys could in fact destroy him…

No, that was preposterous. Chrys would never do that… at least not premeditated. After what we saw her do to Poseidon, I knew it was possible for her to snap and kill him. Man, what I would give to see her do that again.

Persephone said. "Ares knows where to find her, just ask him."

Pothos rolled his eyes. "Yeah, uh, no. I don't think he wants to be seeing me soon, not after what I did."

Persephone held up a hand. "I don't want to hear it. Everything that happened was centuries ago. No one holds you responsible, not anymore. Besides, most of it was Zeus' fault anyway, so both of them might help us because of that."

"Just because you say that, doesn't mean Ares believes it. I don't know if you have noticed, but he likes to hold a grudge or two." Pothos added.

"Well, hopefully you can run faster than him. And if all else fails, Prometheus has the liquid of Lethe that will make him forget that he saw you."

"Would we want to use it for his sake, though? This stuff is scarce." Prometheus held up the vial. It seemed like he went nowhere without it. I supposed he just wanted to keep it safe. Pothos seemed to trust him, so I decided I should too, even though it took months for him to come back on his first quest to help Chrys.

Persephone shot him a look. "You do whatever you can to not fuck this up, okay?"

She could be an actual mom when she wanted to. She had both the sass and the whole snapping-her-orders-to-people thing down real good.

"Yes, ma'am." Prometheus added with a little snark. "You know I'm older than you, Persephone."

"And you know it was us gods of Olympus that put the titans in their place? Just be grateful you aren't chained down in Tartarus with the rest of them. Fuck this up and I will call my husband to do just that."

Prometheus was silent, as were we all. Persephone was scary when she ran out of patience. Although, at this point, I was used to it. She used to erupt like this at Hades all the time. Then have make-up sex...

Took everything to get those sounds out of my head.

"But why couldn't we have talked to Aphrodite earlier? Shouldn't we have discussed everything, make sure she was on our side, before waiting until last minute?" I asked.

"Gods are fickle. If we planned with her, she might have said yes and then gone back on it at the last minute, or Zeus may have gotten the truth out of her. No, we had to wait until the last moment so she couldn't betray us. We will force her to decide on the spot."

That made sense, and I couldn't argue with it. I wanted to, but I didn't have any other points.

"What if she threatens to tell Zeus?" Pothos asked. "What then?"

"Then Prometheus will have to use that elixir. And you leave her and act as if nothing happened."

"But how do we get to Olympus then?" I asked.

She sighed. "We will have to figure out something else. Maybe I can get someone on the inside, but it will be hard. I don't know who to trust, not anymore."

"What about your mom?" Pothos asked. "Couldn't she get us in?"

"No, she is already pissed I never told her about Chrys. I don't think she will help us, especially since she is always kissing Zeus' ass."

I remembered my encounter with Demeter. I understood more about why Persephone was the way she was. She had a mom that had been badgering her for centuries about running away with Hades and how it destroyed her. Demeter, and most of the gods, didn't think highly of Hades since he stayed in the Underworld and didn't enjoy dealing with the drama. With the constant nasty talk about her husband, Persephone, didn't know how to deal. It didn't matter now, all she cared about was saving Chrys, and that was what mattered to me.

"We will figure something out." Prometheus clapped his hands together. "But first, it is time for you to go pick up your daughter."

Persephone nodded. "Yes, I guess it is. I just hope she isn't too pissed still."

I wanted to tell Persephone that she wasn't, but honestly, she probably was. Knowing Chrys, she liked to hold grudges like all the other gods. Then again, she might have forgiven her mother after she let me use her ring to sneak into the Underworld.

"Good luck, Persephone. Tell Chrys... that I love her," I said.

I was expecting someone to make a comment about me admitting that I loved her out loud like that, but no one did.

"I will, Huntley, don't worry." Persephone turned. "Now let's go sirens."

With that, they left the flat, leaving the four of us behind. I let out a deep breath.

Pothos put his hand on my back. "It will be fine, as long as everything runs smoothly."

"Yeah, how many Greek stories do you remember ever running smoothly?" I asked.

Pothos paused for a minute. "Let me get back to you on that."

"Yeah, that's what I thought."

"There is a lot of us that are on Chrys' side and want to screw over Zeus. I think everything will be fine." Prometheus took a seat on the couch. "We will find the angry guy and hope he will help us find Aphrodite. Then we will head to wherever she is and we will get into Olympus, got it?"

"He has helped us out before, I think he will help us find her." I glanced around. "Right?"

Everyone shrugged. Pothos commented. "I suppose. Hopefully. Maybe. As long as we don't piss him off."

Ares was the god of war, I guess it made sense he always had a hot head. It seemed strange to me that he and Aphrodite used to be a couple, as she was the goddess of love and he was the god of war. I guess what they said about love and war was true, that they were more intertwined than people realized. I felt bad for Ares though, as his love life was screwed up by Zeus as well. I could understand the need to seek vengeance against Zeus. Zeus fucked with everyone's affairs.

If he was, in fact, in charge of most wars, I wondered what the world would have been like if he and Aphrodite were a couple. Would there be fewer wars, or did it not work that way? Was it just humans feeding the gods, or were the gods forcing their hand on humans to do their bidding? It wasn't like we ever discussed this theology in school, as theology only looked at the Christian god and how he viewed the world through the Bible. Greek mythology was barely even believed in anymore, and yet here I was, standing in a god's living room.

Life was weird sometimes, if not most of the time.

"Do we know where Ares is now? I mean, he was in London a few months ago, but what about now? Would he stay around this long?"

Prometheus shrugged. "If he is, I know where he would be." Prometheus checked the time. "It's only nine, he's likely at the bar he frequents, drinking as always, then waking up hungover and angry at the world."

So like a normal Brit.

"Which bar?"

"Oriole. It's only a couple of stops on the Underground."

"Then why are we waiting?" I asked. "Let's go."

Prometheus was right, the bar wasn't that far at all. As we entered, my mouth dropped. This was not the type of bar I imagined Ares to hang out in. I was expecting one with pool tables, a fight breaking out, a few broken pool cues. What I wasn't expecting was fancy vases, marble counters, and drinks that I would never have afforded when I was alive. No, this was way fancier than I could have ever imagined.

But sure enough, he was sitting at the bar, drinking what appeared to be some kind of Japanese themed drink with Japanese art on the side of the glass and sushi on top of the glass. I didn't even know where to begin for questioning that drink. I could see Persephone visiting an establishment like this, but Ares, the one who beat up all those guys a few months ago… not so much. He was literally sitting in front of me and I still couldn't believe it.

Although, I had to admit, his nice suit fit in with the style, and his beard was clean and well managed. He was a lot different from Dionysius, who had let himself go.

He glanced up from his drink and shook his head.

"Nope, no more help for you guys."

Prometheus took a seat next to him. "Not even if you get to see Aphrodite?"

Ares looked over at him in the corner of his eye. "What are you talking about?"

"We need her to help us, and you most definitely stalk her and know where she's at. Unless I'm wrong?"

Ares said nothing and Prometheus continued. "We need her help. I don't want to get into details here, but if you help us, then Zeus gets what's coming for him."

Ares snickered as he took a sip of whatever he was having. "Like that day will ever happen."

"It could, if you help us."

After a moment, as if considering, Ares turned to face us. He stared into each one of our eyes. "No."

I was getting pissed at everyone being a pain like this. I was about to grab him by the collar when Pothos stopped me.

"I like humans like him," Ares commented. "It's what keeps me in business."

Now I wanted to punch him for that comment. It was because of him I was angry. It wasn't because I was some human that wanted war. I just got angry a lot. Okay, I could see what he meant, but that didn't mean he had to make that insinuating comment.

"I will not help you go up against Zeus. That ship has sailed for me." He took another sip of his drink. "But if you want to visit my ex, I don't see why there would be any reason to stop you."

Ares pulled out a card that had a name of a hotel in French on it. He placed it on the table.

"It's not like I can control what she does, anyway. Have fun, last I heard she was in a foul mood. Something about being told divorces weren't possible for gods, and yet Zeus is making it happen for himself. Or maybe not a divorce, but some kind of separation."

Prometheus picked up the card. "Thank you, you are an enormous help."

"As I said before, I'm not helping. Bartender, can I have another?"

Prometheus stood up and nodded for us to leave the bar, probably before we could give Ares a chance to change his mind.

Chapter 5

CHRYS

I wasn't smiling when I saw my mother waiting for me in front of the gate to Olympus. She tried to keep a smile on her own face, but I could see the worry in her eyes. She didn't look forward to this reunion either.

It wasn't like either of us hated the other, but our relationship got uncomfortable after everything that had happened. Her and father hadn't been on the best of terms when she left, and I didn't talk to her at all. I didn't know what I would do now that I was stuck with her for the next two weeks.

And what to say to the fact that neither of us would see each other for a very long time, if ever. We would switch who was in the Underworld, maybe seeing each other as we traveled, but that would be it. I did it so I knew my father would never be alone, and at the time the sight of her still pissed me off. Now it was just a dull ache in my heart as I looked at her.

Hermes brought me up from the Underworld, as he was one of the few who could travel between the Underworld and Olympus freely. He blindfolded me part of the way so I couldn't tell father how he got in and out. I thought it was funny, and unnecessary, but he insisted. Once we got past the entrance, he took them off, and I got to watch as we flew through the sky towards Olympus. It was beautiful and bright and… way too bright. I was not used to this much light all around me, so I put on some sunglasses.

If Olympus was anything like this, I would go blind.

Hermes was a lot less chatty than Charon, which was a blessing, even though I would miss that old bastard. The reason Hermes wasn't talking much though was because he was using his own wings to fly us up, which took a lot of his concentration. I had to admit, though, Charon was fun to hear stories from, even if he repeated the same ones. The stories Hermes told me, however, were stories I hadn't heard, and a heads up for some gods that I might interact with.

As we landed next to the gates into Olympus, which were not what I expected. It wasn't a gate like that of the mortal realm, but more of a force-field made of lightning.

I wondered who could have created that.

As I thought about Zeus, my heart sank even more, making it impossible for me to smile as my mother took some steps towards me. I felt a little bad, but deep down I was still a little mad at her.

I wondered if the stories that Maka told me were true—how Hades and Persephone had been madly in love, but it was outside forces that caused the inevitable falling out between my mother and father. If she truly loved him, though, she could fight all that and stand up for her husband, instead of treating him like trash. I guess it didn't matter. Now here we were, two entire weeks of seeing each other.

"Chrys," she held out her arms. "It is nice to see you. Now I can show you what it is like up here with the rest of the gods."

I hesitated, but figured it was probably an awful idea to not accept her embrace. I didn't want to spend the next two weeks fighting and figured it was better just to make my peace with her and move on with my life.

That is, if Huntley and father didn't figure something out. Or I didn't accidently kill Zeus somewhere down the line. No, that would just bring more trouble, and I wouldn't succeed. I just had to hope the others had some idea of how to stop this mess and not get in trouble.

"Well, kiddo, what do you want to see first? We can go see your grandmother, or we can go to Dionysius' place, although I heard he was hiding out in the mortal realm, so I don't think he's home. His place is always open though, and his wine is to die for, or we could—"

I interrupted her. "Can we just go to my room? I want to put my things away and get situated and all that." I didn't feel like doing things that were supposed to be fun, as coming here was more about losing my freedom than acting like I was free to do what I wanted.

Mother looked a little sad I had ignored all her ideas. "Oh, yeah, sure. We can do all those things later." She pulled out a piece of paper. "I've got your room details earlier. You will stay at the complex I live in while I'm here. Our rooms are close, which is good if you need anything. I think you share a wall with Apollo, which might get loud on some nights, but you have my permission to kick his ass."

"And mine." Hermes added. "Or I can do it for you. Just say the word."

I smiled a little as we headed towards the complex. All the buildings were made of a white clay, the ocean was as blue as the sky above, if not even bluer. It was strange that this place was way up in the sky, through the clouds above the mortal realm. I guess when magic was real, anything was possible. It looked beautiful. If it was not for the impending wedding with Zeus, it might even be serene.

But it still was nothing compared to the Underworld. I mean, it was elegant and all, but Oceanus was a lot more beautiful in its own understated way.

Not to mention, I could see in the Underworld without having to wear sunglasses.

I wanted to say that, but I didn't want to seem like a spoiled brat that wasn't impressed. I was pretty impressed with this place and could see how some gods would never leave. I could see why some wouldn't understand why Persephone left it all to marry Hades, when she loved him I guess.

However, I could tell this would not be a suitable

fit.

Like yeah, I would like to vacation here, but it was so bright and I felt like I would burn. My eyes were even starting to hurt as the sun was blazing down on us. Would it go down like it did on Earth? Dear gods, I hoped so. I didn't think I could stand it all day like that. It was not this bright in the Underworld, and I was very thankful for that. Right now, I just wanted to get inside and hide until the sun went down.

"Hey, who do you have here, Persephone? Is this the daughter everyone has heard so much about?" A guy with sunglasses, shorts, and a chain necklace, showing off his bare skin as he wore no shirt, came over to us. His grin seemed almost smug, as if the situation amused him and everything was an inside joke to him that no one would understand.

Or, at least, that was the vibe I got from him. It surprised me that my mother didn't like him. He seemed like all the other guys she snuck into the Underworld.

"Yes, this is my daughter, Chrysanthemum. Chrys, this is Apollo, the god we were just talking about."

Ah, so this was Apollo. That made sense.

He stuck out his hand. "It is nice to meet you,

Chrys. If you ever need anything—"

"She won't be going to you, Apollo, you can count on that. I won't let her." Persephone snapped. "Don't you dare invite her to your late-night parties either, you got that?"

Apollo raised his hands. "Hey now, I feel you are just being rude. There was a time when you liked to come over on your vacations here. Don't act so high and mighty. I remember you before you even met Hades. Stop trying to act so innocent."

Mother was turning red, and I wasn't sure if it was out of anger or if it was out of embarrassment. It wasn't like I didn't know about her wild past. Hell, she was even like that in the Underworld. She brought different men down all the time. I knew what kind of person she was.

So the red in her face was out of anger.

"Just leave us be, Apollo. I don't need your shit today."

He shrugged and sauntered towards the beach. I watched as he left us. He seemed like a royal dick, but I had to admit he was rather hot and well-built. I guess when one was a god; they had to be perfect.

Mother pinched the bridge of her nose. "Just give him no mind, Chrys, and try to ignore the fact you share a wall with him. But as I already said, if you need to punch him, or even use your powers on him, that is fine by me. Just don't get caught."

"I would advise against using your powers, as you will get caught, but I think everyone would understand if you did," Hermes added.

"Is he that bad?" I asked, glancing back at where Apollo was. "He doesn't seem that terrible of a guy. I mean, maybe a little full of himself but aren't all gods?"

Hermes laughed. "That's what they all say when they see him. Then they get to know him and their tune changes quickly, isn't that right Persephone?"

"I don't want to talk about it. Now, let's head to your room."

We made our way through the maze that was Olympus. There were so many buildings that didn't seem to be placed in any order, but just stacked wherever they wanted. I was bound to get lost easily in this place, especially since I only knew of one home all my life and wasn't used to having to memorize how places were laid out. I just hoped I would be a quick learner, even if it would only be for these two weeks.

Unless we failed, and I had to live here with Zeus during the winter for the rest of my life. Then I would have to deal with these gods all the time.

We arrived at our destination. Mother pulled out the key and opened the door. The place was decorated just as I expected all the places here to be: white, blue, and gold accent everything. It was still all too bright for my eyes. I wished I brought more of my décor from home. I guess I could use my powers and redecorate the place if I wanted. I would debate on it as I wouldn't want to get too comfortable in this place.

"What do you think, sweetie? Do you like it?" Persephone asked.

I glanced over at Hermes, who knew me better than my mother. He knew I didn't like the brightness of it. Anyone who had ever been in my room would know that.

"Yeah, it's great," I lied. I would just deal with it, it was the easiest path. I didn't want to get into it with her, not when she appeared to be trying her best.

"Well, I'm glad to hear that. Why don't you make yourself at home and rest up? Then you can meet some of my friends later tonight who are all dying to meet you."

"Yeah, sure, that sounds great," I lied again. I didn't want to meet any other gods.

Persephone clapped her hands together. "Okay, I

will see you in a couple of hours then. I'm two doors down by the sea if you need anything." She turned to Hermes. "Hermes, will you accompany me? I wanted to talk to you."

He nodded. "Of course. Chrys, I hope you can make yourself comfortable. Just yell my name if you need anything."

I nodded, and they both left me standing there in my new room. I let out a lengthy sigh and unpacked my things that contrasted with all the colors that the room comprised. Looking around again, I shook my head. I hated these colors. I hated this place. I hated the fact my mother thought I would be happy here.

To be honest, I knew she was only acting like she thought I would like it here. We both knew the genuine reason I was here and wanted to hide that fact. From her perspective, though, I could understand wanting to introduce me to her friends —I was a long-kept secret that none of them knew about. Now she could tell them about her daughter —a daughter with the god they all made fun of and hate.

This could only end one way, I just knew it.

Chapter 6

HUNTLEY

Why did gods always make everything more difficult?

I sat next to Pothos as we rode in the back of the train towards Paris. Right now, we were going through the tunnel that went under the Channel, which was freaky. I tried not to think about the fact I was under an enormous body of water for thirty minutes. I hadn't even been in a tunnel this long before, and I did my best to distract myself.

Except the only way I could distract myself was by thinking of Chrys, which made me even more anxious. I couldn't win.

I didn't understand, though, why one of these gods couldn't just snap their divine fingers and transport us to Paris instantaneously. No, we always had to go the long, cheap route. I learned that last time, when we went up north to find Dionysius, but that didn't mean I wasn't still pissed about it. Granted, I didn't have to pay for any of it, but it made little sense that they would buy dinner every night and eat out, but for travel, we were in the back with the punks and extensive families. Persephone was always living in style, yet Prometheus always got tickets that sucked. And why didn't Pothos just use his money to get better tickets?

"It's so the other gods don't notice us." Pothos commented, as if he could tell what I was thinking.

"What?" I asked, not sure what he meant.

"If we rode in first class, or took some fancy route, we would be more likely to run into one of the gods. But this way we wouldn't be spotted. Make sense?"

It did, actually. If we were in first class, there was a high probability someone we didn't want to know what we were doing would see us and tell Zeus. I didn't quite understand why no one said that earlier, but now it made sense. And if someone used their powers, Zeus could sense that too. It finally all made sense.

Why did they never tell me the entire reason behind their plan? I swore they enjoyed watching me be all frustrated. I was just their little human pet that they liked to tease.

"So be thankful we planned ahead and understand how everything works. If it was just you trying to save Chrys, there would be no way any plan would work," Prometheus added.

I shot him a look. "I'm the only one who knows how to get through the Underworld, though. You wouldn't have been able to get whatever Hades had for us if it wasn't for me."

He shrugged. "We would have figured out something. Surprised you didn't fuck it up though, especially with Hermes down there and all."

I didn't want to bring up the fact that Hermes caught me. Luckily, it seemed like he was on our side. I wasn't sure why, as from all the stories they had told me, Hermes and Hades did not get along. Did he just not like Zeus? Was he sick of the way Zeus treated everyone as well? Or maybe he got to know Chrys and decided that perhaps she was worth helping.

Yeah, that was probably it.

The train came out of the tunnel and light poured into the train car. I blinked a few times, trying to adjust to the sudden brightness. I was happy to see the sky and never wished to do that again, even though there was a possibility we would come back to London.

We got to our first stop where we had to switch trains to go to Paris. We packed light as we didn't except to spend more than a night or two. I just had my backpack, which I felt was easier to travel with versus a piece of luggage. Now I had both of my hands free if I need to fight anyone. And it was harder to steal since they would have to get it off my arms versus just snatching it from my hand. Granted, I had heard of people cutting away bags and running, but I would like to see them try.

Once we boarded the train, Prometheus said it was only another hour or so until we arrived in Paris. I sighed and bought some chips from the snack cart, which were called crisps here. I still wasn't used to that. Luckily, our attendant spoke English as I knew very little French. The rest of the gods knew how to speak French, though I figured they knew all the languages that humans spoke. They had to understand the prayers and thoughts of people all around the world if they would help them or curse them.

I watched as we passed by the countryside. Farms went by and I wondered what it would be like to live a life on a farm, and whether it would be calmer than what I was going through now. I felt that any life was calmer than dealing with the gods like this.

It was clear when we got to the outskirts of Paris as the density of housing greatly increased and I could barely believe my eyes. The architecture was beautiful, with old gothic style churches and cafes on every corner. As we slowed down into our station, I noticed that the roads were rather dirty, even more so than they were in London. Everyone talked about how beautiful Paris was, I had never heard of how it was so dirty.

I grabbed my belongings and followed the others as they headed towards what was Paris' underground. As we entered the station, we noticed a sign in front of the stairway.

"Another bloody strike. You have to be fucking kidding me!" Prometheus rubbed his temple. "Every other week, I swear. That is why none of the gods come here anymore, it's inconvenient. These humans need to figure their shit out, it's annoying!" He kicked the stand, and I watched as his shoe dented it. Prometheus mumbled some things under his breath about humans never agreeing to anything, which I found ironic given the circumstances. I decided not to bring that up, though. We were all on edge, and I didn't want to add to the problem.

Rubbing his temples, he gestured to head down the street. "I guess we will walk. It's only a mile off."

"Definitely could be worse," Pothos added. "And at least it's nice outside."

I looked up at the sky. It was clear with just a few partial clouds, and a bit warmer than London. I agreed it could be worse.

"A walk will be nice." Mel wrapped her arms around Prometheus' arm. "I enjoy taking strolls through Paris."

"Could we go a little faster than a stroll?" I asked. "I mean, we only have so much time to get to Olympus."

Mel turned around and stuck her tongue at me as we started down the street. I rolled my eyes but said nothing. I didn't want to be on her bad side, as she was scary in her own right, and I didn't like arguing with girls. They always seemed to win in the end.

I tried to enjoy the pleasant day outside, as it had been a while since I got to feel the sun's warmth on my skin. I just wished it was less crowded, as that always made enjoying nature a lot less fun.

"If you feel we might get separated, you have my permission to hold my hand." Pothos gave me a smile. I rolled my eyes. Of course, he was joking at a time like this, it was the only way he knew how to cope, I figured out after spending months with him. He joked as much as I had an anger outburst.

We made our way through the streets, Prometheus leading the way. Mel seemed to be pointing at every lingerie store that we passed, but Prometheus didn't seem to care. Glancing at some mannequins, I wondered what Chrys would look like wearing them.

"Thinking about Chrys?" Pothos asked with a slight grin.

I elbowed him, as I hated it when he looked at my desires. "Shut up, what did I tell you?"

"I didn't read your thoughts, I just saw how you looked at the stores. I can put two and two together. Although…" He paused, then gasped. "Oh my gods, you didn't!"

This time he read my mind. I took a swing at him, but he dodged it.

He laughed. "Ha! I can't believe it. Oh man, I wish I could see Hades' face when he finds out you defiled his daughter. He will be so pissed."

I could feel my cheeks blush, which was surprising since I never did that. "Not so loud, I don't want the others to hear. And he… he found out. I was hiding in the closet when he came in and he noticed right away."

He covered his mouth with his hand. "Oh no… Oh no, how are you still alive? I'm surprised he didn't throw you straight into Tartarus for that. He is not a god I would want to piss off."

"He didn't want to deal with it, not with everything going on. I'm a little scared for what might come later, though, when all of this is over and he decides he wants to discuss it further."

Pothos let out a chuckle. "Call me up after the confrontation. I'm curious if you survive." He glanced around. "But you should buy her one of these, I'm sure she would like it."

I looked around again. I wasn't so sure of that, but I knew she would definitely look good in the black laced one. I shook my head. No, this wasn't a time to get stuck in my fantasies. We had to find Aphrodite right away.

It wasn't long before Prometheus stopped in front of a hotel. It was tall, but looked like it was built in the 1800s. There were flags all on the outside and as we stepped inside, the entire place was made of fine marble and granite. Damn, it would have been nice growing up rich. Maybe I wouldn't have had as many problems as I did when I was human, although my parents caused most of my problems, anyway. I doubted money would have changed that.

Prometheus stepped up to the front desk and spoke in fluent French. He made Mel stay back with us as he flirted with the girl. Mel looked pissed but knew sweet talking the receptionist would be the best bet in getting him to tell us the room number. After a few moments, Prometheus came back over.

"She is on the top floor in the grand suite. I got us a key. Luckily, she has been having men come and go, so it was easy to convince the receptionist that I was one of those suitors."

Mel wrapped her arms around his waist. "And you are just that charming."

"Let's get going then, before they realize it was all just an act." I said, hoping the receptionist didn't notice Mel all over Prometheus. If she did, she might not think he was with Aphrodite and call security.

Heading towards the elevator, Prometheus led us up to the top floor, which this building only had eight. I was surprised, as it had seemed taller than that on the outside. A few moments later, as the elevator was rather slow, the doors opened to show us a hallway with only a few doors.

Apparently, all the rooms on the top floor were spacious. Hell, they looked like they were larger than the trailer my parents had. That they might still have.

We stopped in front of a doorway, and Prometheus pulled out the keycard. He slid it and opened it.

"Wait, shouldn't we knock first?" I asked.

He shook his head. "No, she isn't here, she is out shopping like she normally does. Then she will go out for dinner and then she will get back and we will be waiting."

Pushing open the door, he was clearly shocked to find out he was wrong. There, in the middle of the room, stood Aphrodite with her arms crossed in front of her chest.

Prometheus forced a smile. "Aphrodite, long time no see."

She did not seem happy to see him.

Chapter 7

CHRYS

This sucked so badly.

At least it was dark now and I could see all the stars. They were beautiful, even though I thought the shimmer of Oceanus was a lot more beautiful. The night sky was tranquil too, I supposed. It was better up here than on Earth, there was no pollution here.

As for getting along with my mother's friends, I didn't find that to be easy. I loathed the couple of hours I had spent with them and just wished to be back in my room. At least Hermes had hung out with us and kept me company. He and I would make comments to each other either about a god, or reference something funny that happened in the

Underworld, and laugh to ourselves.

The others didn't care for it.

It wasn't like they were terrible people, they just were preoccupied with themselves for me to care about what they were discussing. First it was about makeup lines, then about how humans were rude when cutting in queues, and so forth. It wasn't stuff that I cared for, or felt was important. It was all superficial stuff that I didn't quite understand why a god would care.

There was a reason my father didn't leave the Underworld, and I was seeing why.

Hermes didn't seem to have a problem talking about some stuff they brought up. I guess he was used to this crowd and could talk like them. I had a feeling he didn't enjoy it as much as he tried to act like he did, though.

Currently, we sat around a campfire on the beach with the three sirens my mother introduced me to, Demeter, my grandmother; along with Apollo and a few of his nymphs. I wasn't sure how Apollo became part of the group tonight, as mother kept telling him to leave and ignoring him, but he was here. I tried to stay clear from him, as something about him made me shudder. It was like he was intimidating both physically and sexually, and something about that made me scared and a little excited.

He mainly talked with the nymphs, which were two girls and three guys. All five of the nymphs seemed pretty talkative, but I was too far away to hear. I also didn't want to hear, as Apollo offered me a smirk every time I glanced over. I had to look away every time. With him around, I was losing the ability to be inconspicuous, if I even had that talent.

As for my mom and her three friends, I wasn't sure how I felt about them. They were all sirens—creatures that haunted the waters and killed men that dared to even look at them. I mean, that was metal and cool, but they weren't as punk as I would think creatures like that would be. Instead, they were a lot like my mother and kind of bitchy, to put it mildly.

And really, really scary.

Then there was my grandmother Demeter. I could tell she didn't like me at all. She glared at me a lot. If I tried to say something, she would turn her head and act like I wasn't there. It was great. It didn't matter; it wasn't like I wanted to befriend her or anything. She was the reason my father and mother had marital issues—she was the reason that my mother could only be in the Underworld for three months. If it weren't for her…

I tried to shake away my anger towards her out of my mind. There was no use for exploding in her face right now. I would probably never see her over the next few months, and it didn't seem like she wanted to see me, anyway. I was just a bitter reminder of how her precious daughter ran away with the man she loved. No, Demeter didn't think my mom loved him. She thought Hades had kidnapped her against her will.

Deep breaths, Chrys. You are not like them—you could hold your temper, especially since when you lose your temper, you almost kill someone. Or did kill them over and over again.

The beach here was warm, even at night, which felt great on my skin. I was neither sweating nor shivering, and the beauty of the night sky reflecting on the waves was rather marvelous. It smelled salty and sweet, and I wished I could enjoy it by myself. Instead, the scenery was ruined by all the surrounding people. I stared into the fire, wishing I was back in the Underworld, or just to disappear from this place.

Was it bedtime yet?

Hermes slapped my back. "Hey, you know what?

You haven't ever seen the full moon in this place, have you? It is about to rise and is beautiful on the sea."

I shook my head. "No, I haven't seen it."

"It should only be about an hour from now, and we have plenty of s'mores to last us a while."

I didn't want to stay around for that much longer, but I had a feeling that I wouldn't have a choice. I also wanted to see the moon come out. Everything was so clear, unlike in the city. Was this what the Earth was like centuries ago? Before human inventions plagued it?

"I won't say no to another s'more. Pass me the marshmallows."

Hermes passed me the marshmallows, and I put one on a stick to roast in the fire. I tried not to let it catch on fire, which is what Hermes did every time. I thought it was interesting how it seems like most of the gods were impatient for the minor things, which was funny when they lived for such a long time. I guess when you had all the time in the world, you got bored.

Once the marshmallow was a perfect crisp golden brown, I placed it between two graham crackers with some chocolate. All the ingredients were substantial and boasted strong flavor. I wanted to eat all of them, but also didn't want to stand out amongst the others. Other than Hermes, no one was eating anymore. Mostly, they were just drinking some kind of alcoholic beverage exclusive to Olympus. I had a bit, and it tasted like peaches and cherry with a hint of apple.

Time passed and much the same happened. I was staying quiet as all the rest were talking among themselves. Hermes and I had a lot of fun making s'mores at least.

The moon came out, and the light shimmered on the water. I gasped in astonishment as the whiteness of the moon was a lot more beautiful than the sun ever could be. I wished it was nighttime all the time. Then everything wouldn't be so bright.

"The moon is beautiful," I commented. "Why can't all of the worlds be as beautiful as this all the time? The sun is too bright, but the moon is perfect."

"You mean shrouded in darkness just like your father likes?" Demeter commented. It shocked me, as she had barely even spoken to me this entire time.

"Mother," Persephone started, but Demeter held up her hand.

"This girl shouldn't exist, nothing should ever had been born by Hades. And of course, she is some goth freak, loving the night and darkness. No god or goddess should love the darkness, not in the way they do. They just bring death and destruction wherever they go. Zeus is a fool to think she should belong up here, even if it's only for three months of the year. He only thinks with his dick."

"Mother!" Persephone stood up. "Don't you dare talk that way to my daughter!"

I was surprised my mother would stand up for me. It made me like her just a tad more at that moment, but what she had to say after made that spark quickly go away.

"She is not like her father! She is not dark and brooding like he is. She is funny, smart, and can achieve great things. She may be able to bring death to this place, but she can also bring life. She is my daughter, after all, she just needs to learn."

I frowned. Father wasn't dark and brooding, he was fun and liked to play games and cared about the people he ruled over. He made sure everyone in the Underworld went where they needed to go and that they had a joyful life after death, as long as they deserved it. Sending people to Tartarus wasn't a simple task, the people and creatures there had to have a genuine reason for going there. Even I had sent people there when I helped my father judge.

He had been doing it for centuries and had never lost his cool, or his sanity. I doubted any other god could do the things he had to do.

I stood up. "May I be excused for the night?"

Persephone paused, then nodded. "Yeah, go ahead."

Leaving them there, I hurried off to my room. I could feel everyone's eyes watching as I stormed off. I had to get out of there before I did anything drastic.

Luckily, I was able to figure out the maze back to my little apartment. The moon was bright now and it lit up the pathways enough where I could see where I was going. Hermes was right, it was bright and beautiful. It was larger than I had seen in the human world.

I wished Huntley was here to enjoy it with me.

Taking a deep breath, I entered my room. At least with it being dark, I couldn't see the ugly décor. Collapsing on my bed, I slammed my face in the pillow. This sucked so badly. Not only did I not have Huntley to talk to, but I also didn't have my father here to hug me when I was down. I had Hermes, sure, but I still wasn't sure I could trust him, at least not with sharing my inner thoughts. He worked for Zeus, not for me. He cared more about getting this wedding done than in helping me.

"Ugggghhhhh!" I yelled into my pillow. After taking a deep breath, I glanced over at the music box. I had ten pomegranate seeds in there. It wasn't the end of the first day and I already wanted to take that sweet drug. Ugh, what was I becoming?

I had to face the fact that my grandmother hated my guts and wanted nothing to do with me. Then my mother talked shit about my father…

Yeah, maybe I deserved a pomegranate. I just would promise myself I wouldn't have another for a couple of days. I would want to save up for the next two weeks, and maybe longer if I did in fact have to marry Zeus. It was all stuff I didn't want to think about, so I popped open the music box and took one seed.

I sat down on my bed, waiting for it to take effect as I stared out at the moon's reflection in the water. It was so beautiful, as its white light shimmered on the black water. I wondered what it would be like to swim in it right now, as the depths were darker than ever. The only time I had ever been in water that deep, and that dark, was the night Poseidon tried to drag me into the River Thames. The whole fight became a blur once the water filled my lungs and choked me. Then everything seemed to go black until I was hit by that lightning. That was definitely a loud wake-up call.

I felt euphoria as the seed's effect spread through my body. All my muscles seemed to relax as a slight buzzing went through my body. The colors of the moon shifted, and everything had colors dancing all around. I took deep breaths, wanting to stay in this state forever. It felt like bliss.

Listening to the waves hit the sandy beach sounded like a song only nature could have provided. I rocked my body back and forth to it, although wishing I had brought some metal music to listen to. That was always the best, as the loud screams and fast-paced music made it even more sensational.

As I sat there, I thought I heard a few howls. I glanced around, wondering what in the heck it could have been. It was a full moon, yes, but were there wolves in Olympus? I didn't think there would be. I guess I didn't know the area that well.

There was another howl. This time, it was loud, almost like it was coming from within the complex. I didn't know what to do, and in my state of mind, I wasn't sure if everything was playing a trick on me.

Slowly getting up, because that seemed logical at the moment, I crept over to the door and cracked it, seeing if I could get a peak of whatever was going on. There, in the hallway, were a couple of wolves.

"What the fuck?" I whispered, not sure if they were there or not. Was it just my imagination or were they real? And why would they be out here in the corridor, even if it was an outdoor corridor? And why was no one else noticing them? Was this normal?

One wolf looked over at me, and in an instant, smoothly transformed into Apollo. I fell back, surprised, and my door creaked open all the way. He laughed as he leaned against the doorway.

"Curious, are we?"

"No, I just heard wolves and got confused. Didn't know if it was in my head," I said as he helped me up. I tumbled a bit as I was still under the effects of the seed.

"Whoa there, what have you been up to in here?" He studied my eyes. "Yeah, you've been taking something. Pretty strong too. Got anymore?"

I shoved him away. "No, now get out of here, I didn't invite you in."

He grabbed me by the wrist and pulled me out into the corridor. "There, I'm no longer in your room."

I tried to pull my wrist out of his grasp, but he

was a lot stronger than me. "Let me go."

"Why don't you come join us, Chrys? We have a lot of fun. I can teach you therianthropy. It is one remarkable experience, especially when you are drug-induced."

I heard a loud smack. Apollo let go and grabbed the back of his head.

"Bad dog!" Persephone said as she held a rolled-up magazine. "Leave her alone and get to your room or I swear I will end you myself."

He waved her off and went back towards his room, swiftly turning back into the wolf he once was.

I started back for my room when my mother stopped me. "Chrys, wait, are you okay?"

Nodding, I opened my door. "Yeah, I'm fine. Don't worry about me, it's not like you ever did."

With that, I closed the door behind me and sighed. That was a complete buzz kill.

Chapter 8

HUNTLEY

Aphrodite was not happy we were there. I wasn't
sure if it was because she had a beef with Pothos, or
Prometheus, or because she knew why we were
there. I had a feeling it was all three combined.

Her dark brown eyes glared at us, and even
though she looked furious, she was beautiful. Her
coffee-colored hair was curled perfectly, as if it was
just something natural she woke with. She wore a
deep green silk dress that contrasted with her olive
skin. I could see why she was the goddess of love,
she was beautiful.

But not as beautiful as Chrys, though I wouldn't
say that out loud. Pothos told me about the Trojan
war, and I would not make that mistake.

Prometheus stepped forward, forcing a smile. "That was a long time ago, can't we just forgive and forget?"

She shook her head. "No, you made a fool of me, you asshole!"

He sighed. "It was a complete misunderstanding. I thought you knew Ares would be at that fling. I thought you wanted me to invite him."

She stepped forward and slapped Prometheus across the face. The smack was loud and sounded like she made full contact. Prometheus took it, though, and didn't retaliate. But he flinched a little, and a red mark appeared on his face.

Aphrodite shouted. "No, I didn't! It's been hard enough dealing with my marriage with Hephaestus. Then you pulled that stunt! You know Zeus found out about it and thought I was trying to run away with Ares, right? I was in deep shit for decades! All because of you!"

"Look, I'm sorry. I acted rashly. Okay, I was just —"

"And you!" She pointed at Pothos. He flinched, thinking he would get slapped. "You were part of his scheme too! You both were just trying to get me in trouble with Zeus so you two could get him off your own backs. You might as well just leave because I will not listen to any shit you two tell me!"

Aphrodite shoved us back towards the door when I stepped forward. "Wait, will you listen to what I have to say?"

She just looked at me for a moment. "And who the hell are you?"

"My name is Huntley, ma'am, and I need your help to stop the wedding between Zeus and Chrys, the daughter of Hades."

She laughed as she looked me over again. "Excuse me? Why in the world would I ever help you? Besides, did you just hear what I said about Zeus? I am back on his good side. I don't know if you know this, but he is the god of gods and you don't want to piss him off, otherwise there is a lot of shit to pay. Hear that? I. Am. Not. Going. To. Help. You. Now leave me be."

I didn't budge. "No, you will help. Persephone said you would help us get into Olympus. That is all you need to do. Zeus will never know it was you and you will be fine."

She laughed. "Are you kidding me? He always knows, isn't that right, Prometheus? I'm surprised you would go along with this shit after how he tortured you for centuries. Do you want to go back to having your insides pecked out every day?

Because if not, then I would stop this little charade of yours. It will only cause torture and chaos for anyone who was seen talking to you. Again!"

"Aphrodite, how about you just take a deep breath and listen to what we all have to say?" Mel stepped in. "There's more to this than just the wedding. It's way out of Zeus' tyrannical rule."

She shook her head. "You are joking, right? You think anyone can stop him? It isn't possible."

Prometheus explained. "Chrys can kill any god. She has the power over death and rebirth. She is Hades' daughter—his actual daughter. She is the one from the prophecy of bringing down the gods of Olympus, if given the chance."

Aphrodite let out a sigh and shook her head. "You realize that prophecy could include any god from Olympus, right? Including me? Do you think I would want to help someone who might destroy me? Go find someone else."

"There is no one else." I yelled. "We have been working on this plan for months now and you are the only one who can help us! Persephone came up with the plan, and she said you were our best bet!"

She raised an eyebrow. "Persephone? You think she cares? She hates the Underworld. And she had a daughter down there to go back to and she still loathed going there. Doesn't that say a little something about her?"

I had to admit, she had a point. "It doesn't matter, she has been helping us and I really think this plan will work if you just hear us out."

She shook her head and lifted her arms. "I said get out."

Suddenly, I felt my body being pulled out by some invisible force and all four of us were on the ground in the hallway as the door slammed shut. Glancing around, I found that everyone was surprised she would use her power to kick us out.

I slammed my first on the ground. "Are you fucking kidding me! Why can't anything ever go as planned!"

"Welcome to the club," Prometheus commented as he stood up. "Nothing ever goes as plan when gods are involved."

"What should we do then? Should we try again or should we go somewhere else? Is there even someone else we can talk to?"

Prometheus shrugged. I glanced over at Pothos and Mel. They didn't make eye contact with me. "What, are you all just going to give up?"

"No one is saying that." Pothos dusted himself off. "We will just have to think of something else."

"Let's all go get some coffee and rethink this through. Besides, I still have her keycard. She didn't seem to think anything of it, so perhaps she won't get the code changed when we try again."

I sighed and decided not to argue about going to get coffee. It had been an interminable day and some caffeine would help. I also was curious what coffee in France would taste like, since they were big into it like England and tea.

It wasn't hard to find a shop close by and we all took a seat inside near the back corner. Pothos ordered for me as I did not understand what anything said other than "café." He ordered me a noisette, something that he thought I would enjoy. Although I didn't care to go out for fancy things like they did, I appreciate it every once in a while. It was something that I would have never even been close to getting when I was alive. I decided instead of being the typical punk and ignoring such things to take pleasure in the splendor while I could. Few could say that.

Our order came out, and I took a sip of the noisette. It was strong, really strong, with very little milk. It came in one of the small cups that usually had the pure espresso which I found to be very overpriced. At least I didn't have to pay for it. It was good, though, smooth and strong. I would have to pace myself, though, so my heart wouldn't start racing from the caffeine.

If I ever came back here with Chrys, I would definitely have her try this. I think she would enjoy it as much as I did, if not more.

I placed the cup down. "So what are we going to do now?" I asked.

"We wait." Prometheus took a sip of his drink and looked out the window. "For the one person who can get through to her. There is a reason I picked this coffee shop, and it's because we can see her window from here."

I looked back over at the hotel. He was right, we could. I didn't even realize it. "So she knows we haven't left the vicinity. Great."

He shook his head. "No, she doesn't look down here that often, and if she did, it wouldn't be for us."

"What do you mean?" I asked.

Pothos nodded. "There he is. Look."

I peered down the sidewalk where Pothos pointed. Ares stood there, looking up at the window. It would have been the perfect movie shot if it was also raining.

"But he was just in London. Why would he have

come out now?"

"Because Ares has a soft spot for a love story," Pothos commented. "But I didn't tell you that, got it?"

I wanted to ask what he meant by that, but decided not to. "Okay, so we just need to get him to convince Aphrodite to help us?"

"It isn't as easy as that," Mel commented. "Even if we get Ares to help us, that doesn't mean Aphrodite will side with him. If you didn't notice, it pissed her off that we tried to set them back up a little while ago. If she sees Ares with us, she is going to be really pissed again and think it is a trap to get her in trouble."

"Why would she even get in trouble? Don't you gods always have affairs and sleep with other gods?"

Pothos shrugged. "Yeah, but Zeus is a dick so sometimes not all of us get to do that. And some don't even get to have sex, as they have sworn to chastity, although I feel that is so Zeus can't try anything with them."

"So first we need to get Ares to side with us. Let's focus on that first," Prometheus said. As he set his cup down, Ares turned and entered the cafe. "Quick, everyone act like they don't notice him."

Really? We were playing that childish game? I sighed as I turned to study one painting on the wall. It was of a flower. It was yellow. Cool.

Ares ordered an espresso and once they handed it to him, he came straight over. "I know you all were watching me. I'm not stupid."

Prometheus tried to act surprise. "Oh, Ares, I had no idea you were in the country, let alone Paris. Who would have guessed?"

"Shut up. Tell me, what did she say?" Ares pulled up a chair and sat down at the table.

Prometheus shrugged. "Mostly what I expected, she is pissed at the three of us, and doesn't care about Huntley's plea since, well, he's human. She doesn't want to go against Zeus."

"I don't blame her."

"I don't know how to get her to side with us," Prometheus went on. "And even if you sided with us, I'm not sure she would help. She seems really freaked, I have no idea what he did to her those decades after that party."

"He put her in isolation for a while, some tropical island or something. Don't get me wrong, it was a nice island, but there were only some humans on it and she wasn't allowed to talk to any of the gods."

That didn't sound like a punishment to me, but I

guess for them it was.

"If we succeed, though, he might not even be ruler of Olympus."

Ares raised an eyebrow. "You think this young goddess will able to get rid of him? I thought your mission was just to stop the wedding, not to kill Zeus."

Prometheus shrugged. "We will see. It's all up to Chrys."

I wasn't sure what Prometheus meant by that. The point was to save Chrys, not to get her to fight Zeus. That was never mentioned in all the meetings we had, yet this was twice now he pointed it out to other gods. Was it because he was trying to get them to side with him? Hoping that their hatred for Zeus would get them to help if they thought he would die?

I said nothing as I just wanted these gods to help. I didn't care if Prometheus lied as long as we got Chrys back.

"Besides Zeus gone, what is in it for me?" Ares asked. "Not like I care if that fucker is alive."

"Isn't it obvious?" Prometheus asked. "If there is no Zeus, then there is no reason for you not to marry Aphrodite. She could get a divorce and come back to you."

Ares shook his head. "She doesn't want me, not anymore."

"I beg to differ." Pothos smiled. "I can see into people's hearts and she still loves you."

Ares studied him for a moment. "Fine. I'll see what I can do."

Chapter 9

CHRYS

I still wasn't sure if everything that happened last night actually happened.

Laying there on my bed, I took a deep breath and tried to sort out what was the pomegranate seeds and what was real. I could just ask my mother if she did in fact hit Apollo in the head with a magazine, but then she would question why I had to ask that. I could lie and say I thought maybe it was a dream, but there was also the fact I didn't want to talk to her unless I really had to. I could also just go next door and see if there were a bunch of wolves passed out. That would answer my question, but I also didn't think I wanted to see that.

Sighing, I glanced out the window at the sun that

shined ever so brightly. I swore it had risen earlier than normal just to spite me. I couldn't sleep when it was lighting it up in here—I was not used to such light while I tried to sleep. It wasn't like I wanted to get up either, not when all that was out there waiting for me were stuck-up, sex-driven gods and goddesses. Then again, they were up late last night and probably weren't awake yet. I could have the entire neighborhood to myself.

Deciding to check if I was right or not, I changed into some clothes—typical black pants and a dark purple shirt, and headed out to investigate.

Glancing around the alleyways and down the beach, I found no one to be seen. My theory was correct. I could use this to my advantage. Maybe not today, as I wasn't ready, but I found a way I could sneak out of here for later. It was dead quiet and morning had just broke. I could escape this place if I wanted, or at least it appeared like I could.

Since I knew I wouldn't be interrupted, I wandered around to see if there was anything interesting in these areas. Mother had only taken me to meet my grandmother, whom didn't want to meet me, and her friends yesterday, so today I could get a better idea of what this area was like.

There were a lot of apartments in Olympus, all of

which seemed to be occupied. I wondered who used to stay in my room before I came. Maybe I didn't want to know. As I walked through the alleyways, I found all sorts of creatures lying against the walls, passed out drunk from an interminable night. Was this what it was like every night? Was this all the gods did? I felt my heart race. This was not a life I belonged to. I was more of an introvert like my father, not someone who could party all night long, night after night. I couldn't belong in this place, I would be miserable for so many different reasons. Mainly, having to be with Zeus, but this was just salt in an already festering wound.

I took a deep breath and went through everything in my head. Should I try to run away right now? It wasn't like I saw any guards in my vicinity, and Hermes was nowhere in sight. Curious, I made my way to the entrance and found no one guarding it. Were they not worried any unwanted people who might try to storm Olympus? I guess most humans didn't believe in such a place, and there hadn't been an enemy of the gods since before my time. Maybe they had nothing to worry about.

Until I came along.

Apparently, I was an enormous threat, and that was why Zeus wanted to keep me close. I was surprised I hadn't seen him yet, especially since he seemed so keen on making sure I didn't cause trouble. I was also glad I hadn't run into Poseidon, but I figured that was because he ruled over Earth and he would stay in his domain. He would probably be at the wedding though...

Yeah, I had to find a way out of here, quick.

Taking another deep breath, I tried to calm myself down. There were not enough pomegranate seeds in the universe to make this tolerable. I couldn't go through with it—I could not stay here for another second.

I made a decision with myself: I would try to escape the next morning. I could go back to the Underworld, no one would find me there. Father could hide me somewhere, and no god other than Hermes could come looking for me. The Underworld was an enormous place. It would take him a long time to find me, if he even could. I could stay with Maka, or maybe even Nyx. I hadn't seen her in a long time, but I was sure she would help me.

Heading back to my room, I decided to wait around until someone came and got me. I didn't particularly want to run into any gods without my mother or Hermes there. Although I wasn't pleased to be around my mother, at least I knew she had my back when I needed it, at least when it came to dealing with the other gods.

I quietly snuck by Apollo's room, not wanting to wake him for fear of dealing with his shit again, if that in fact happened. I doubt he was up this early though; he didn't seem like a morning person which seemed odd since he was the god of the sun.

Laying back down on my bed, I closed my eyes and tried to picture Huntley. It had been a while since I had last seen him, but I could still picture his every detail in my head: his shaggy, almost curly, cocoa hair, his wide smile that always made me think his lip would split, his hazel eyes and strong arm that held me close.

I missed him so much.

I regretted making him stay in the mortal realm, but it was the easiest decision given the ramifications of him being anywhere in the vicinity of Zeus. If he was around, I knew that I wouldn't have been able to face all of this, not to mention that he might concoct some type of escape plan better if he was away from me. If he were in the Underworld, Hermes would have known everything that was going on. This way he could sneak around with Prometheus and the others. I knew the gods had Huntley's back—they hated Zeus that much.

At least, that's what I hoped.

There was so much going on right now—much of which I was kept purposely out of the loop, but I just couldn't stay still any longer. No, I had to get out of here and either find them or go hide somewhere. Hiding sounded better, as Zeus didn't have control over the Underworld—he despised the place. But I wondered if it would still put my father at risk. No, Zeus wouldn't actually go after his own brother, would he? On Earth, Zeus showed me he would fight to the death with Hades, but if I was missing, could he blame my father? Only if Zeus knew for a fact that I was there, which he wouldn't. He didn't know everything that was going on Earth either, so that meant that I could even hide in the mortal realm, if I tried my hardest. Maybe some secluded island somewhere in the tropics? Or the desert? Or the Arctic? Anywhere was better than here.

Getting up, I opened the window and let some fresh air in. It was a pleasant morning, not too cool but still not at the heat of the day. A gentle breeze entered, smelling of salty beach air. This part of Olympus I could get used to—the smell of the ocean air filling my lungs, and the cool air caressing my skin. This would be paradise, if it weren't for the gods living here, and the sun being so bright. If it were dimmer, and I was by myself, it would be perfect.

I heard a knock on the door and wondered for a moment if I should answer it. I didn't want to talk to anyone, and I hoped it wasn't Apollo. The only people who knew I was on Olympus, besides him, were mother, Demeter, those sirens, Hermes, and Zeus. If I answered, the odds were that it would be one of those people. I didn't have anything to fear, other than a couple of them, 70% of them at most. If I waited, maybe they would say something through the door.

The person knocked again, not alerting me to who it was.

Well, if they weren't pounding on my door, that meant they probably wouldn't kill me… Probably.

I got up and opened the door. A woman stood there, her arms folded, and shooting daggers with her emerald eyes. Her blonde hair was wavy, almost curly but not quite, which laid gently against the white halter top she wore. She even had white pants and boots to match. It was the complete opposite of my entire wardrobe.

"Uh, who are you?"

She shoved me forward into the room. "Leave my brother alone!"

Her brother? What the hell? "I have no idea what you are talking about!"

"Apollo! I saw you last night! I can see everything the moonlight touches and I saw the way you were looking at him on the beach! And last night in the corridor, I saw you try to go into his apartment. If your mom didn't stop you, who knows what could have happened. "

Was this woman a lunatic? "What the fuck? I did not look at your brother all night, and I did not want to go in his apartment!"

She shoved me again. "Yes, you did! All the girls swoon over him and I wish you would all just leave him alone!"

I shoved her back. Yeah, I was stooping to her level, but who could blame me? I didn't see any other possibility. "No, I didn't! Your brother is a fucking pervert trying to back me into a vulnerable position!"

"How dare you!" She screamed as she jumped on me, scratching and punching. "My brother is the light and sun and would do no such thing!"

I tried to get her off of me, but it was no use, she

was strong. At least, I got a few elbow strikes into her gut and she backed away for a second.

"Get away from me!" I yelled as I got up.

She ignored my request and pulled out a knife.

Well shit.

I scanned the room for anything that would work as a weapon, but I had nothing. We went around in a circle as she measured me up. What the hell was wrong with her? Did this seem like a logical thing to do to someone you had just met? Heck, we haven't even met, and I had no idea who she was, yet here she was, trying to kill me.

"Look, I don't like your brother, like at all! I'm Zeus' fiancé and I wouldn't be stupid enough to have an affair under his roof. Right? So no, I didn't try to have sex with your brother last night."

She paused, as if this was all news to her. "So, you're the infamous daughter of Hades?"

And here she said she saw everything the moonlight touched. "Yeah, I am."

"You are the one that killed and revived Poseidon over and over again?"

"Yeah."

She nodded. "I saw that, it was quite impressive. It even made me laugh a little. But that doesn't change the fact that I want you dead after what you tried to do last night."

"Oh my god! Just listen to me, will you? I didn't try to sleep with your brother!"

She charged at me with the knife. There wasn't anything I could do to stop her. I wasn't much of a fighter other than with my powers, and I didn't have any weapons in the room with me. That only left me with one option.

I had to use my powers and pray that no one notices.

I wasn't going to kill her, but just hit her enough to let her understand I was for real, or maybe just knock her out. When she was close enough, I grabbed the wrist that had the knife and focused my power on her hand. She screamed as she let go of the knife. Black marks stretched through her veins from where my hand held her wrist.

"What the hell! How dare you!" Hypocritical coming from the person coming at me with a knife.

"You started it! Now stop before I use any more of my powers, got it?" I asked as I threw her wrist down. She held the wound on her wrist and started for the door. She stopped for a moment, as if pondering.

Please don't do what I think you are about to do.

She leapt towards me, screaming again. I shook

my head as I held up my hands to defend myself. It wasn't my fault she was asking for it.

I brought my energy together and was about to knock her down when the door flew open. Before I knew it, Apollo had her flung over his shoulder.

He gave me a little wink. "Sorry about that. Artemis gets a little protective of me. She will be out of your hair now, don't worry."

"Like hell I will!" She screamed, kicking, and punching Apollo as he carried her out of my room.

I stood there, not sure exactly what had happened. All I knew was that I definitely would get out of here tomorrow morning.

Chapter 10

HUNTLEY

There was no way that this was going to end well.

After talking to Ares, we somehow decided to all visit Aphrodite's room together. I did not understand why any of us thought that would be a marvelous idea after what had happened earlier that day. She made it very clear she wasn't happy with any of the gods here, especially, well, all of them. It was also clear she didn't want to see Ares as Zeus had punished her for their love affair. I wondered if Ares also had been punished for their affair. I had a feeling the answer was yes, as Zeus seemed to like punishing anyone he could. If that was the case, though, I wondered what Zeus made him do.

Prometheus slid the card through the key reader, and the door, to my amazement, opened. I thought she would have got a new key card for the door. Maybe she wanted us to come back, or she didn't think about it. As he opened the door all the way, something hard and large hit the door, sounding as if it broke into a bunch of pieces.

"I said get the fuck out Prometheus!" Aphrodite shouted at us. "How dare you come back here! Do you want me to call the police? Because I will!"

I wondered if she meant the human police or if the gods had some secret police, they called, if gods weren't leaving them alone. Either way, I didn't want to find out.

Prometheus opened the door just a little more so he could see her, but still kept Ares out of view. "Just hear me out! If you don't like what I have to say, then we will leave you alone."

She folded her arms in front of her, as if defeated. "Fine, I'll listen, but you have one minute, so make it quick!"

Prometheus grabbed Ares by the arm and threw him in the room and closed the door. I blinked. I did not see that coming, and neither did Ares because he looked like he was trying to spill out all the cuss words he knew at once, but Prometheus had closed the door before any of them came out. He pulled the door shut as Ares tried to open it, not moving a budge.

Prometheus turned to us with a slight smile. "It's fine, he will calm down in a moment. Or punch through the door, either one."

That sounded promising. I leaned against the wall, opposite to the door, and listened as Ares pounded and yelled for Prometheus to open the "god-damn door", which left me having that Panic! At the Disco song stuck in my head.

Prometheus could hold the door closed, even when going up against the god of war. I was pretty impressed. I mean, Prometheus was strong and all, but I had a feeling Ares was even stronger. I concluded that either Prometheus hid his strength and was stronger because he was older, or that Ares wasn't trying that hard. After a few moments, during which it surprised me that no security came running up here because of all the noise and security cameras, Ares gave up and there was silence.

Prometheus let out a breath. "Okay, I think he calmed down, but I will hold the door here just in case. He's tricked me before."

Oh great, this wasn't the first time Prometheus

had done this. That was promising.

I closed my eyes and listened. So far, I heard no more yelling, not even from Aphrodite. This surprised me, as she seemed to be a loud person, although that was because she wasn't being heard. She didn't want to deal with Zeus if all this backfired, and I couldn't blame her. I had seen what Zeus was capable of, and besides Chrys at her full power, I didn't think any of the other gods could take him.

"How long do you think they will be?" I asked.

Prometheus gave me a critical look. "You are so impatient. This may take a little while."

I didn't mean it impatiently, rather if we would simply stand here the entire time. How would working out their relationship help us? Would Ares stand up for us and talk her into it? Or would he feel betrayed and not help us now?

I slid down the wall and sat down on the floor in surrender. I might as well get comfortable here since I was already getting stiff, and we had walked so far earlier today. Pothos took a seat next to me.

I turned to him. "You think she will listen to him? Hell, do you think he will still help now that we tricked him?"

Pothos shrugged. "Who knows? She seemed

angry earlier, but once Ares showed up, she stopped yelling and throwing things. I think he might get through to her. As for Ares…. I think he will still help us. He has nothing to lose at this point—she is his everything."

I could feel for Ares, as I too had my love taken away by Zeus. In my case, though, I still had time to save my love, and he could eventually have his.

Prometheus seemed to lessen his grip on the door and let out a deep breath. "Okay, I think he calmed down. They are facing the inevitable and talking about everything."

Mel put her ear to the door. "Yeah, it sounded like they are talking. Normally too, no yelling."

"That's good," Prometheus ran his fingers through his hair. "I was afraid they were just going to turn their backs on each other and keep silent."

Melinoe shook her head. "No, they are definitely talking."

I was glad to hear that, especially since it seemed like they didn't want to talk to each other beforehand.

Pothos had said that they were originally a couple, but then Zeus decided to give Aphrodite away to Hephaestus. She pleaded not to marry him, as she didn't love Hephaestus, and found him to be grotesque, which I had no idea because I had never met the man. It was a little hard to believe any of these gods could be ugly, as all the ones I had met were beautiful. Even Hades was pretty handsome.

Ares had been broken since the breakup. He gave up once she left him and Ares became even more hellbent on creating wars. It was why the wars themselves seemed to get bigger each and every century. Personally, I think Zeus should let Aphrodite leave Hephaestus so that Ares would stop the wars. But apparently gods didn't think things through when it came to humans, or they just didn't give a rat's ass.

A few moments later, the door opened. Prometheus stood in a ready stance, prepared to take down Ares if need be. Ares glared at him from the doorway. I didn't think I wanted to see this fight if one did in fact break out.

"Aphrodite says she's ready to talk if you, that is, if you have a plan to stop the wedding and hurt Zeus."

Prometheus nodded. "We do."

Ares signaled for us to come in and we took the invitation and entered the room. Aphrodite was sitting on her blue sofa, appearing as if she had been crying a little.

I glanced around the room. Now that I was actually in here, I could examine the room. It was nice, really nice. It was the nicest room I had ever seen, even after going to Fortnum and Mason's that one time. Other than the broken vases in the entry area, the room was clean—nothing out of place. Everything felt perfect, and I felt as if I did not belong in here. Just looking at this stuff made me think I would accidently break something.

"You have five minutes. Go." Aphrodite stared at Prometheus straight in his eyes.

Prometheus brought his hands together in a clap, ready for this moment. "Hades has given me the tools used in the Underworld to declare a marriage with Chrys. All we need to do is to get to Olympus to find his daughter and complete that ceremony to show that we are already married before Zeus' marriage. Zeus can't refuse by his rules, and we play pretend for a while. Then she will have more training in the Underworld on just how to use her powers. When the time comes, we can take down Zeus once and for all."

Aphrodite was silent for a moment, taking in all the info that Prometheus had given her. I watched as she glanced at each of us and finally spoke. "That's it? That's your plan?"

Prometheus didn't falter. "It's the best one we've got and is the best shot we have had in centuries."

Aphrodite sighed. "And what makes you think Zeus won't still just take her anyway? That he will actually follow his own rules he put into place? I don't know if you have noticed, but he doesn't tend to follow his own rules."

Prometheus was silent for a moment. He shrugged with a half-smile.

Aphrodite rolled her eyes. "Yeah, that's what I thought."

"Everyone will be there," he spoke up. "He can't go against everyone at the same time, especially Hades. He will have to follow his laws. Besides, Zeus likes virgins and with this we can get him to believe she isn't one."

I felt my face redden as Pothos glanced over at me with a smirk. I knew I would punch him if he said anything at the moment. I didn't want the others to find out, not with everything going on. I didn't know if it would complicate things, not to mention I didn't want the others to make snide comments. I admitted I didn't regret it in the slightest, especially since it was the most amazing thing I've experienced in my life and death. I didn't think I could go on living if I didn't have her in my life again. She was my everything.

I wondered why they assumed Chrys was a virgin. Was it because there was no one else in the Underworld, or was it because Pothos could read her passions and see that she had never acted on her feelings before? That was before I went down into the Underworld, of course, and he had only just found out about the two of us.

A thought occurred to me—why was it Prometheus who was the one who had to act as if he was marrying her, or had already married her? Was it because he was a god, or titan, or whatever, and I was just a mere human that he wouldn't care if something happened to me? That had to be it. It didn't seem like the gods cared what humans did, but only cared about themselves when it came to rules. Unless one of them wanted to fuck a human. That was when things got heated and shit happened. I didn't quite understand that logic, but it was logic none the less.

Man, I wished I paid more attention to the teacher when we were going over mythology in Global Studies. Maybe I would understand this intricate world better, but then again most couldn't understand how these gods interacted, and how they were still alive. I wish I could get some of them to reveal all their secrets and then explain how they were still alive. I wondered what chaos would ensue when put on the spot.

"I can't get you into Olympus, I lost my guest privileges a while back when I snuck Ares into my chambers."

Prometheus shook his head. "That makes little sense, Ares can go up to Olympus whenever he wants. Why would you lose your guest privileges?"

Aphrodite rolled her eyes. "I don't know, it's Zeus, he doesn't think about his punishments. And then as you know, Ares isn't allowed to bring anyone after the complete fiasco with those vampires."

Now that was a story I wanted to hear. Ares let a brief smile appear on his face. Oh, I really wanted to know more about that later.

Aphrodite went on. "But I can talk to Hera, and she might be able to do something that will get you in. She also is a ruler, so she can bring in anyone with no trouble."

Prometheus laughed. "You think you can get Hera to help us?"

She gestured with her hand. "Why not? She has ruined every other conquest of Zeus', why not this one?"

Prometheus folded his arms. "Because she

punishes the woman, not Zeus himself."

"But this way, she can stop the wedding before it happens and give Zeus the finger. If I talk to her now, she might calm down and think it through."

I had heard the stories of how Hera had turned some women into creatures, or just outright killed them. Those were all humans though, Chrys was different. She could fight back, especially if she could take down Poseidon.

"If she would do anything to Chrys," Pothos began. "She would have done something by now, especially since Chrys is already up there. I don't, however, think she wants this wedding to go through. If she has calmed down about everything already, she might have a cool enough head to help us."

All of us nodded in unison. It made sense. It seemed like if the gods would act, then they would act fast. I doubted she would hurt Chrys, especially after how she had hurt Poseidon so badly. I wondered if she was okay in Olympus right now and whether the other gods were giving her a hard time.

Dear god, I hoped not. Or else Zeus might just end it there, or have the wedding earlier than planned. I hoped neither of those things had happened already. Otherwise we will have lost her already. Reversing marriages was a task that just didn't happen for the gods. It would only be for three months of the year, yes, but I still didn't want Chrys to go through that.

"Fine, I will contact her. It's about time I go back up anyway, otherwise my husband might be upset, and I don't want to get him upset." She held herself tightly, as if thinking of what he might do.

Ares went to her side and placed her arm around her. "You don't have to go back if you don't want to. I can protect you." He kissed her cheek. "Fuck Zeus, he shouldn't get a say in other people's business."

She turned to him and placed her hand on his cheek. "No, I need to do this. If Prometheus succeeds, it might be a chance for us. I will go for that."

Prometheus nodded. "Thank you. Please send Hera to our flat in London. I will leave you two to be together for a bit, as I can see you need it."

They didn't turn away from each other as we left. Well, I guess that went well this time.

Chapter 11

CHRYS

I had to get fitted for a wedding dress. It was the most awful thing I had to endure, and I knew that it was only the start if I stayed here.

Excluding Apollo. That was a whole different level of awfulness.

I stood there in front of the mirror as my mother watched. Neither of us were smiling by this point. She had been smiling at first, trying to be excited for her daughter's wedding. I was her only daughter—a wedding should be joyous. But as the day went on, that smile vanishes as the realization what all this was about sets in.

This wedding wasn't something to be excited about.

Also, the gods in Olympus had horrible, horrible tastes in colors and fashion. Wedding dresses, apparently, weren't white up here but red and yellow. And I hated red and yellow together, more than I hated the color white. It clashed, at least for me. I wanted to wear black, or a deep purple that matched the sky at night. But instead I was wearing clashing cloth that was draped over my body.

And the veil was red, which just increased my anger because now I was literally seeing red.

"You look…" Mother tried to be positive, but I could tell she was pushing it. "Great."

I gave her a look, then turned back to the dress designer. She was a wood nymph, with clothes that were far more stylish than the ones she was putting on me.

I asked, "Is it possible to wear different colors? These don't seem to fit my style."

"Nonsense," the nymph said. "These colors are traditional! Every goddess wears them when she gets married."

I looked over at my mother, who shook her head. Of course, she didn't wear these colors. She got married in the Underworld. She probably got to wear black. And black wasn't even a color she liked anymore.

I let out a sigh. "Whatever. I don't care."

"What are you talking about?" the nymph asked. "You are marrying the god of all gods, you should be the happiest goddess alive!"

I gave my mother another look. She didn't respond, but took a sip of her fifth mimosa. I could not wait for the next morning to come so I could get out of here. I had everything ready and decided just to leave shit I didn't care about behind. I would only take a light backpack and just make a run for it. It didn't seem like anyone could stop me, and they hadn't questioned me when I was wandering around earlier this morning if anyone had seen.

Once the nymph was done with the wedding dress, or what she called a wedding dress, she brought out an entire chest full of jewelry. All of it was shiny gold, some ordained with bright rubies.

"Damn," I said. "What's all that for?"

She smiled. "This will line the entire dress. But first, we need to pick out what you will wear as a necklace, and a tiara, and earrings, oh and bracelets."

Maybe I would just make a run for it right this instant.

My mother didn't say a word as she downed the last of her mimosa. A nymph brought her another one.

"Thank you," she said.

"Is the jewelry necessary? I mean, the dress is… striking… enough."

"Nonsense, you need to stand out like the shining sun! You will be the wife of Zeus! Oh! That reminds me." She pulled open a drawer. "We should practice your makeup."

My eyes widened as I turned to my mother. She held up her glass. "Want one?"

The fiasco was over and I stared at the makeup that was still plastered on my face. This would take a lot of alcohol to get off. My eyes were surrounded by red powder, lips even brighter, and gold flakes covered my skin.

"How is the bride-to-be? Is she decent so can I look?" Hermes walked in with his hand over his eyes. I laughed a little, glad to have someone I liked pop in to see me. I still had only my underwear on, but I grabbed a robe and put it on.

"You can open your eyes now." I said.

He opened them and his mouth dropped. "What the hell is wrong with your face?"

"This will be my makeup. You just missed the dress."

"Aw man, that's why I came all the way over here."

"Don't worry, you didn't miss much," I whispered. The nymph gave me a look, and I rolled my eyes. Not my fault the colors she picked were ugly.

"She looked beautiful," Persephone answered, her words a little slurred from the seven drinks she had consumed. She leaned in and whispered something to Hermes. He chuckled.

"What?" I asked.

He shook his head. "Don't worry about it. You will look amazing."

I rolled my eyes again. No one would look good in that atrocity, especially now that it would be covered in emeralds. Why were the gods so bad with fashion? This dress wasn't something anyone would wear in the last few millennia. It was strange to me they would keep such customs since they liked to see the mortal world and shop around. A lot.

"What are you doing after this?" Hermes asked.

I shook my head. "I have no idea, ask my mother."

He looked over at her. She answered. "Nothing is planned. Do you have an idea, Hermes?"

"Well, I was thinking we could go check out this new gelato place in the center of Olympus, over in that new shopping district? You know the one I'm talking about Persephone?"

"Oh yeah, I had heard about it. What do you think, Chrys?"

I shrugged. "Sure, why not?"

I mean, I liked gelato, so I wanted to go check it out, I just couldn't show that to the two of them I was excited for anything in Olympus. Hermes knew me well enough, though, and he knew I had gelato almost every day. It also surprised me to hear there was a whole shopping district up here. Was it like the mortal realm in that it had a city and places to shop? It was a little strange to think of a city made just for the gods, especially seeing as we created everything we needed in the Underworld. Conjuring did the trick.

The nymph finished picking out all the things I needed for the wedding, and I would try the entire ensemble in a week. Mother thanked the nymph, and I tried not to make sarcastic comments the entire time. Hermes then led the way towards the center of Olympus.

Ugh, it was so bright outside. I put on the sunglasses my mother bought me this morning, along with the black sunhat.

"You know, you look like you are on the way to a

funeral."

I gave Hermes a look, then realized it was hidden underneath the sunglasses. "Well, I consider this to be my funeral so I guess it's fitting."

"I suppose that is fair. I just meant that you will get more people staring at you than I would think you would want."

I shrugged. "At this point, I don't care. I'm my father's daughter, after all. I assume this is how they looked at him the few times he came up here."

"Yeah, I suppose you are. And yes, it is the same look. You two are almost identical. I can't believe there's some Persephone in you as well."

Persephone elbowed him in the ribs. "Hey, she is my daughter! You can tell in her beauty and spunk that she takes after me."

Hermes laughed. "Yeah, I suppose there's that. But she has her father's attitude, that much I learned in the Underworld."

"I can't believe you made it out alive, Hermes. Hades has always wanted to stab you for all your jokes and mischief."

"Oh, he tried. I think if it weren't for Chrys, I would be dead by now."

"But you wouldn't have been in the Underworld for that long of time if it weren't for me anyway," I commented. "So he wouldn't have stabbed you."

"Yeah, I guess there's that." Hermes smiled.

Glancing around at the scenery, it surprised me how much it looked like Greek coastal towns, as the white clay buildings made up the entire city. Some were even two to three stories tall, but other than that there weren't many tall buildings. It all covered up a hill with an enormous palace at the top. I assumed that was where Zeus lived.

The shops were very diverse. I saw one that was selling decorative pots while the one next to it sold some fashionable hats, and so on. They were all so specific, and it seemed like you could find anything in the greatest quality here. It was a wonder why any of them bought stuff from the mortal realm, knowing the mortal realm's reputation for wear and tear.

Maybe the fact it was made by a human made it unique? That was my only guess. And perhaps the natural deterioration was seen as a curiosity.

"Here we are!" Hermes gestured to a building that looked much like all the other ones, other than it had a sign for gelato. The layout of the city was a complete maze, and I wondered if I could find this place again without Hermes' direction, not that I was staying long enough to come back here.

We ventured in and found the place to be busy. Everyone was here to try the new gelato parlor, which I didn't blame them. gelato was the best.

I glanced at their menu and found that they had a lot of unique flavors, including bone marrow with smoked cherries, kale, peaches and cherries with chocolate shavings, but one stood out above the others, and that was the honey lavender. It sounded so good and while it wasn't the most unique flavor, nothing beat honey. Or lavender.

"Know what you want?" Hermes asked as he pulled out a couple of gold coins. I was stunned and didn't realize the gods had currency. I wondered how it worked since it wasn't like many of them had 9-to-5 jobs. Were they given an allowance by Zeus? I had no idea since we never used the currency in the Underworld.

"I will take a scoop of the lavender honey." I said.

"Want to add anything to it? You can also get two scoops if you wanted."

I glanced at the menu again. That didn't even occur to me I could mix and match. "Can I get Earl Grey as well?"

He laughed. "Yeah, you can."

Hermes ordered the gelato, and mother picked rose with pistachios. That also sounded good, but I didn't regret my choice. I took a bite and felt as if I was in heaven.

Oh wait, I kind of was…

We got a seat outside and watched as different gods, nymphs, and creatures walked around. I wondered what all their stories were, and how they got to be in this place. I had been around so few people while living in the Underworld, so seeing so many unfamiliar people was strange to me, or at least being in the middle of so many different immortals. I saw the afterlife for humans and creatures alike, but it wasn't the same as being in the middle of it all.

"You know, Chrys, you got the same gelato that I have seen your father get." Hermes smiled as he took a bite of his double chocolate chip.

"Really?" I asked. "I didn't know he had a favorite gelato. I mean, I guess he would, but I haven't seen him eat it that often."

Hermes pointed his spoon at my mother. "Yeah, when you two first met, wasn't it at that old gelato shop that used to be by the entrance of Olympus? You and him kept running into each other there."

Persephone shrugged. "That was a long time ago, I don't remember what he used to order."

Of course she didn't. She didn't care about father

like she used to, if she ever used to.

"I'm pretty sure I'm right, I mean my memory is perfect."

"I'm sure it is Hermes. A lot better than mine anyway."

Not much more was said as we finished our gelato. I had to admit, though, it was one of the best gelatosI had ever had. It was creamy but not too rich and it didn't melt and get all over the place like it normally did, even though it was a lot sunnier here than it was back home. I wondered if that was because gods and not some staff that father had hired, who served some time in order to get into a better afterlife, made the gelato. I sort of wondered if that was considered using his authority for his own benefit, but never questioned it. It all seemed fair to me.

"See," Hermes said as he took his last bite. "This place isn't so bad."

"I opened the door to find my neighbor had turned into a wolf and am sure he was having an orgy. Then his sister tried to kill me this morning because she thought I wanted to sleep with him."

Hermes just stared at me, then laughed. "Oh Apollo, why do you torment your sister like that? He knows she can see anything the moonlight touches, yet he stays out and does shit like that."

"The fact you think that is normal scares me," I said. "And it's something I don't want to have become normal for me."

"Welcome to the club, kid. Now you see why your father hides so much."

"I just don't see why you all put up with this shit. And then think my father is odd for wanting to stay the hell away from it all!" I got up and slammed my fist on the table. "It is annoying as hell. You all think it's fine to make fun of him, yet you are the ones that are all crazy!"

I started to storm off when my mother grabbed my arm. "Wait, Chrys."

I jerked my arm away. "No, you are the worst one of them all! You don't stand up for him and treat him like shit! You are the one he loved most and you don't even care!"

Running off, I hoped I wouldn't get lost in the maze-like layout of this place. I figured it would be okay, because if all else failed, I could just ask someone where Apollo lived. Seemed like a lot of the gods knew of the place since he hosted parties often.

I also didn't care if it took me a while to get back, as I wanted to be alone in my thoughts for a bit. I hated this place and just wanted to go back home to the Underworld. If I didn't understand my father before, I did now.

I wasn't sure how much time had passed, but the sun was just about to set when I got back to my room. It was quiet, as everyone seemed to be out doing something else. I slammed my door shut and gathered some of my things and put them in my bag, including the music box. Nothing would stop me from leaving in the morning, not even if it was Zeus himself.

Chapter 12

HUNTLEY

The next day we returned to London.

Never again will I share a room with Pothos. He talked in his sleep and damn was it graphic. It was like reading someone's sexts, and I really didn't want to read someone's sexts when I was trying to sleep. All I could do was think about Chrys the entire time, and that kept me up all night. Luckily, I could catch up on some of my sleep on the train, even if the stiff chairs weren't all that comfortable.

But now we were back in London, and Prometheus made me go walk around outside as he hated it when I paced inside. They all did. It would probably be a couple of days before we would hear from Hera, as Aphrodite had to travel up to

Olympus, find her, and then talk to her. All the others said I was lacking in patience and needed to get my mind off of it by exploring London some more. I swore that I had explored the entire city now, even the Underground, which I wouldn't recommend since the cops did not like people wandering down there, even if some of the tracks weren't used anymore.

This time, I decided to go check out a comic store that I had seen the last time I was out. It was called Forbidden Planet and Pothos gave me some cash so I could get something to read. It had been so long since I had read a comic, that I wouldn't even know where to start. At least that would give me something to do.

I took the Central Line to the Tottenham Court Road exit. The train was rather packed, per usual on the Central Line. It seemed like most people took this line to get to wherever they were headed for the day. I would think since it was close to afternoon that there would have been fewer people, but I supposed since there were so many tourists that that wasn't true.

I got off at my exit as the door opened and wandered the streets, knowing the direction I needed to go but not in a hurry to get there. There was also a bookstore near it that was rather huge, but I decided I'd rather get a graphic novel instead as I loved seeing the art.

The place was surprisingly packed. Comic book stores when I was alive were rarely packed and often closed down since they didn't get any patrons or a certain online megastore had forced them out of business. I wondered if it was because many tourists came here since it was rather large, or if it was because there were a lot more comic-based movies out now. I had seen a few of them, as Pothos collected a ton of films. They were all pretty good, and it was amazing to see what film producers could do now with special effects. It would have been cool to see them when they first came out.

I still couldn't believe there were new Star Wars movies. Crazy how many things could change.

I made my way into the basement where all the graphic novels were and gasped. There were so many, I didn't know where to start. Maybe I could just get a classic X-Men? I found the Marvel area and saw how many X-Men comics there were. Oh my god, were there always this many? It was crazy to even see so many series and crossovers, let alone try to catch up with all the latest of each. Were there people who had read all these? And if so, I had to give them props because that is some major commitment.

"Can I help you?" A worker who looked about my age, or at least my age when I died, asked. He could tell I was overwhelmed.

"I came to buy some comics, but have no idea where to start."

"What kind of comics do you like?"

I shrugged. "Action ones, I guess? I grew up on X-Men Evolution and the original X-Men cartoon. Other than that, I don't know what's out there."

"Well do you want to stay with Marvel or would you be interested in any indie comics? Or manga?"

"Manga?" I asked. I did not understand what that was.

"Japanese comics."

Oh man, that was a thing now? I remembered Sailor Moon growing up, but that was it. "Are there many mangas?"

He laughed. "Yeah, there are a lot."

"Uh, I don't know."

"Let's stick with comics. One of my favorites if you like comedy is Deadpool versus Dracula. Deadpool and Gambit is also good. I feel you would like Deadpool and he kind of breaks the fourth wall, so you can read them separately from the rest of the

Marvel universe usually."

He handed me a couple of his favorites to check out.

"Let me know if you need anything else."

"I will, thank you."

With that, he started helping a different customer. I read the backs of the comic he suggested and found that the Dracula and Gambit with Deadpool sounded the best. Gambit was also one of my favorites growing up, so I knew I would like it. It was a pity he wasn't in any of the recent ones.

I purchased the two comics and as I glanced outside, I saw a familiar face.

"Son of a bitch," I mumbled as the cashier handed me the rest of my change. I quickly took my purchase, and bolted out the door.

"Hey you asshole!" I yelled as I ran after the blond-haired man walking down the street. He turned when he heard me, and I knew I had been right. It was A.J.

When he saw me coming straight at him, he bolted like the stupid coward he was. I would not let him get away, not after what he had done. No, he was going to be forced back to the flat, and I would have the others hold him down while I beat him to a pulp.

This was all his fault, and I would never forgive him for what he did. He befriended Chrys for centuries and betrayed her like it all meant nothing. I know I could never live with myself for what he did. And the worse part of it all was that they had rewarded him for what he did and now was immortal, just like a god.

But why the hell was he still here? If I were him, I would have left London as soon as I could. I only stayed around because that was where Prometheus and the others stayed. I would have preferred somewhere tropical and warm. Actually, I would have preferred anywhere where Chrys was, but that wasn't currently possible.

The asshole was fast, but he didn't have all the years of running from the cops under his belt like I had. I was a little faster than him, even if he was a demigod. I could catch up and tackle him.

"Got you, you son of a bitch!" I threw a punch straight into his jaw. He hit the ground, hard. Even if he was immortal, that had to hurt because it sure hurt my knuckles.

I threw another punch and another. I felt like Ares would be so proud as anger raged through me. If it weren't for A.J., I would still be in the Underworld with Chrys and we would be happy and she wouldn't be suffering like she was. She wouldn't have been engaged to Zeus, and she wouldn't have had to make Hades worry like he was now. This was all his fucking fault.

"Okay! Enough!" A.J. yelled. "I get it! I'm sorry, okay!"

I let out an ironic laugh. "You, sorry? What gives you the right to be sorry? You aren't forgiven and you will never be forgiven! You get that? You are an asshole who deserves to be tortured for an eternity for what you did!"

"I know, okay!" He yelled back. "I feel awful and am plagued with nightmares constantly! I never meant to hurt her, I just wanted my life back! If I had known she was as nice as she was, I wouldn't have done it. But it was too late, everything was already set in place."

I just stared at him. "No, that makes no sense, you could have stopped it somewhere, I don't know, perhaps by not egging her on to go to the mortal realm, or just decide not to tell your father in the first place! Don't give me this bullshit that you feel sorry because all of a sudden you have a conscience and want to be forgiven. Some sins don't get to be forgiven, you get to spend all eternity living with what you've done!"

He turned his head to the side to avoid looking at me. He knew I was right and had made a colossal mistake. "Look, I went back to the land that I once ruled, and my kingdom was no longer there. No one even knew who I was."

So that's why he felt guilt. I grabbed him by the collar and shoved him onto the ground again. "How many times did I tell you that? I said that I had never heard of your kingdom and that it was not a place anymore!"

"You were stupid, and I didn't trust you."

I punched him in the jaw again. That's when I heard whistles behind me being blown.

"Hey!" A cop yelled. "Get off of him and stop fighting in the streets!"

I was so glad that cops in London didn't have guns. I pulled A.J. up and forced him to follow me away from the cops.

"Hey! Stop!"

Again, I had a lot of years of being chased by cops under my belt. These cops had nothing on the cops in Philadelphia, especially when you were a punk.

A.J. could have gotten away from me by now if he really tried. Maybe he was feeling regret and wanted me to punish him some more, or maybe for me to forgive him, which wasn't ever going to happen. I wanted to take him back to the flat so that the others could interrogate him. Then I realized, what if this was all a set up and he was in fact spying on us to tell his father or Zeus what we were up to. Now I debated on bringing him to the flat. Maybe I should consult with Pothos before I did anything rash. I would call him after I lost these cops.

We rounded a few corners and didn't hear their yells anymore. We kept running for a bit, though, just to be safe. There were so many people now that he wouldn't be able to spot us.

I reached into my pocket for my phone to realize I had forgotten it. Damn it.

Glancing over at A.J., I thought about what I should do. It wasn't like he didn't know where we lived, as he had been at that party with us. As long as Hera didn't show up, he wouldn't have an idea about what we were up to.

"Debating on what you should do with me?" A.J. asked. I gave him a look. "Good to know you're as violent and straightforward as ever."

"Just shut up, okay? You have no room to talk."

"Whatever, just decide before the cops come back. I don't want to deal with that hassle again. They aren't the best people to deal with, especially when you aren't actually human."

That was very true. Even if we had all the identification cards, there were still holes in our story they liked to find.

"Fine, I'll take you back. But I can't guarantee your safety. They are as pissed as I am in how you betrayed Chrys."

"Oh, goodie. Can't wait."

I led the way as we headed back to the flat. I still miraculously had my bag of comics and was glad I didn't drop it somewhere along the way. Pothos would have been pissed that I had wasted his money. Again. Something similar might have happened one night when I went to get dinner. I may have gotten into more fights these last few months than I cared to admit.

We arrived at the flat and I opened the door to find the three of them still on the couch talking. As A.J., with his bloody nose and face, walked in, he tried to smile.

"Hey guys, look who's back."

Pothos was the first one up, coming over and punching A.J. in the stomach. I thought it would be Mel as she was quicker on her feet, but Pothos was closer. I watched as A.J. cowered into a ball on the ground as Pothos kicked him. Yes, this felt great. I added my own kicks as A.J. covered his face with his hands.

"Enough! Gods, do you guys think violence is the answer to everything?"

I didn't know what the others thought, but I had to say the answer was yes.

Prometheus stood up. "Enough! Let us hear what he has to say. He wouldn't just come back for no reason at all."

Pothos and I got off of him and A.J. rolled over onto his back, coughing up blood.

"Give me a sec."

Prometheus gave him a good kick into his side. "No, talk now!"

"Fine!" He coughed again. "Let me tell you everything I have heard."

Chapter 13

CHRYS

The sun was just about to rise, and I hadn't heard a noise from any of the gods, not even Apollo and his wolf-posse, for a couple of hours. The same nymphs from the night before were over in his room and I heard all sorts of noises throughout the night that I didn't want to hear and hoped to never hear again.

I grabbed my bag and opened the door. I half expected someone to be standing there, trying to stop me or ready to go tell Zeus what I was up to, mainly Hermes as he would always do that in the Underworld. But there was no one. I closed the door behind me and crept down the corridor. I didn't hear a stir from any of the other apartments.

I would get away with this, or at least I hoped. If I didn't, and I got caught, there was no telling what would happen to me, and my father would be furious. He wanted me to run away, of course, but he also didn't want me to die, which would happen if anyone found me.

Meaning I couldn't mess this up, and I had to hide somewhere no one could find me.

The Underworld was still my best bet for where to hide, as Zeus couldn't search every nook and cranny without my father's permission, not to mention it would take a very long time to search all the Underworld. It was an enormous place, as it had to hold all the souls that have ever passed, along with the ones that were to come. Not to mention I had friends down there who would help me out when I needed it.

Looking up at the sky, I made sure that the moon had gone down, especially since Artemis said she could see anything the moon touched. And Hermes made the comment as well. I didn't want to deal with her again. Although it didn't seem that she would care about me leaving, but more if I snuck into Apollo's room. That was most definitely not going to happen again.

I wondered why she had such an obsession about

her brother, and why I had somehow been dragged into the mix. There were nymphs passed out at her house, yet she had gone after me. That made no sense. I also noted that Hermes said Apollo did it to piss off his sister. I did not want to be at that family's next get together.

Luckily, I didn't have to deal with any of Apollo's comments the night before as I had shut myself in the room way before twilight ever came. My mother had tried to come over to talk, but I told her I didn't want to be bothered. I was sick of the way she treated my father, and I wished she was the one marrying Zeus, not me.

Venturing through the maze that was Olympus, I realized I wouldn't miss any of it. Well, maybe the gelato, as that was super delicious, but I could find good gelato again. Everywhere sold gelato. It wasn't like I would go without it. It just might never be as good, but having yummy gelato wasn't worth being married to Zeus for.

I couldn't believe I was just thinking about gelato when there were more important things at hand, such as not getting lost in this maze.

I wondered if I could find the entrance to Olympus, or at least the point where Hermes brought me up. It was dark and everything looked different from earlier. Shit, was I lost? I just hoped no one would wake up to find me out here, wandering about.

Because no matter what I said, it wouldn't look like I was innocent when I had my backpack full of my things…

The sun still wasn't all the way up, as it was still just peaking up at the horizon. It wouldn't be long, though, until it was fully up and I would be screwed. The more time I found myself lost like this was another moment wasted in getting away.

I rounded another corner and let out a breath I was holding. There it was—the opened gate Hermes had led me through from the Underworld.

Surprised it was open, I decided I shouldn't question it, and let it be fate that wanted me to escape this place.

Or maybe there was some magical trap.

I stopped and stared at the gate, now nervous that it did in fact have a spell on it. What if I disintegrated when I stepped through the gate? Or what if I turned into a frog, or a tree, or worse? I bit my lip. Was it worth the risk? Were those things better than marrying Zeus? I stood there for a moment and thought about it.

Yes… yes they were.

I started forward when I felt someone grab my bag and pull me backwards. I screamed and turned around to find Hermes smiling.

"I thought I would find you out here."

My heart was pounding in my chest and I bent forward, gasping for air. "Damn it, Hermes, you scared the living daylights out of me."

"Good, I had to get up at the crack of dawn to monitor you. I hate mornings more than Apollo does, yet here I am, saving your life."

"Saving my life?" I asked. "Is staying here a life worth living?"

Hermes picked up a rock on the ground and threw it at the gate. As it hit it, the rock appeared as if it had been hit with a lightning strike and became ash. So it was enchanted.

Hermes turned to me. "You thought it would be that easy to get out of here for you?"

"So everyone here is held captive? What the hell?"

Hermes shook his head. "No, you have to have a keycard on you to get in or to bring in guests. If you have the keycard, then you don't get zapped."

I paused for a moment. "... What's the keycard look like?"

He pulled out a white plastic card. "Like this. I don't care for the look, but—"

I snatched it from his hands and bolted for the gate."

Hermes yelled after me. "Son of a bitch! Chrys! Get back here with that right now!"

I didn't listen to him but kept on towards the gate. I just prayed to the gods he wasn't joking with me, but was in fact how to not get electrocuted.

Here went nothing.

The gates opened and I was just a few steps away from freedom, when Hermes wrapped his arms around me and lifted me up. "Nope, you don't get to leave today."

I kicked and punched, but he was a lot stronger than he looked. "Let me go! I want to get out of here! I shouldn't be here!"

"I know, I know, but they would hold me responsible for you disappearing and I don't want to deal with that mess."

"At least you won't have to marry him! Just lie and say you didn't see me!"

"Well since I was the one in charge of watching you, I don't think that would work. Besides, maybe I would have to in your absence, you never know."

I gave up on trying to fight him—he was a lot stronger than me. Although I wanted to use my powers, I knew that would be a mistake. I liked

Hermes enough to not want to hurt him. "Why do you even listen to him?"

"Because, I have no choice. Now come on, I will take you to your mother's room."

"What? No, please don't."

"Too bad, I need some sleep after having to watch you for so long. You realize I haven't slept since we got here? I have been afraid you might bolt, and that you might be in danger."

"Then where the hell were you when Artemis attacked me?" I asked.

"I saw Apollo would handle it and decided he could deal with his own sister. Artemis isn't someone I enjoy dealing with."

I let out a breath as he grabbed my arm and dragged me towards Persephone's apartment.

"Watching Persephone hit Apollo with a rolled-up magazine was priceless, though. I wish I videotaped it because I would watch that repeatedly. God, it was hilarious. Just smack right on the head."

So that did in fact happen. I had been so out of it, I wasn't sure. I'm a little glad it did because my mother sure put him in his place.

"So you saw me yesterday looking around?"

He nodded. "Yup, which is why I figured I had to keep a close eye after that."

"You know if you just told me you were watching me, I wouldn't have run."

"I was more curious if you would actually try it. It took some balls to run, as you knew the consequences."

It made little sense, but I didn't want to question him any further. I was pissed he had been toying with me for the past couple of days. I thought he was the one I could trust, but I was wrong—I couldn't trust anyone.

Hermes took me through the city, quicker than I had ventured through it, as he knew the exact ways to turn. He was also in a hurry to make sure no one else spotted us. There still weren't any gods out, it appeared that none of them liked mornings. Were father and I the only ones that would get up early and do their job? If that was true, it wouldn't surprise me.

I was still surprised I hadn't noticed Hermes was watching me this entire time. He had watched me for months in the Underworld. Why would that change when we were in Olympus?

What I didn't like was that he sort of toyed with me to see if I would run away or not. If he had just said something, I wouldn't have tried and I wouldn't have put so much effort in trying to get away, not to mention risk my life. If another god had seen either of us, would I have gotten in more trouble?

I guess I had to be thankful he wasn't going to Zeus with the information that I was trying to run away. He could have just set me up to let me get in trouble with Zeus, and I would have been killed right then and there. I guess that was what made Hermes a trickster god.

We came upon my mother's door and Hermes knocked on it. A few moments later, my mother opened the door, dressed in a white robe.

"Oh no, what did she do?" She asked when she saw Hermes holding me by the wrist.

Hermes smiled. "Nothing special, just tried to make a run for it. I need you to watch her while I get some sleep. I haven't slept in days. Can you do that for me?"

Persephone sighed. "Yeah, I guess so."

I wondered if the sigh was because she didn't want to deal with me or because of everything going on. I figured I didn't want to know the answer.

Hermes pushed me forward then waved goodbye as he headed towards his own apartment. I didn't know what I thought of him now. I understood he was doing his job, but he could have been a lot nicer about it and just told me.

Persephone closed the door, then gestured to sit wherever I wanted. I threw my backpack on the couch and sat down next to it.

"What were you thinking?" Mother asked as she sat down across from me.

I gave her a look. "I was thinking it would be fun to just have a stroll outside. What do you think I was thinking? I want the fuck out of here!"

She let out a sigh and rubbed her forehead, as if I was just a problem to deal with. "You can't leave. No one can disobey Zeus."

I leaned back, my arms crossed. "Yeah, I'm seeing that. You all are too scared to stand up to him. It's ridiculous."

"You just don't understand what control he has over all of us because you have been protected by your father in the Underworld."

I jumped up and pointed at myself. "I don't understand why I can't just stay in the Underworld. It wasn't like I endangered anyone while I was there. All of this is so stupid and I have no way out!"

Persephone tried to step forward to comfort me, but I pushed her back.

"No! You have no right to comfort me! You have not helped me figure a way out of this, not once! You just act like this is all fine and dandy instead of thinking about what I want! Why don't you care!"

"I care!"

I shook my head. "No you don't, mother! All you care about is yourself and what you will wear at the next enormous dinner thing and who will be there and how many drinks you can get guys to buy you!"

"That's not true—"

I let out a laugh. "Yes, it is! Tell me, when have you ever cared about me! When have you ever stood up for me!"

"I've been working months with Huntley to get you out of here!" She yelled. "We have a plan so just stay put for a while!"

We both stood there silent, realizing she had yelled that for all of Olympus to hear. We listened but there was no sound and we decided no one heard what she had said. She let out a sigh.

I whispered. "You talked to Huntley?"

She nodded. "So don't worry and just go along with it all. He and the others have it under control. Hopefully. But running away isn't a choice that you have. He will find you no matter what."

I understood, although I didn't want to admit she had a point. I had acted rash, but could anyone blame me? My neighbor's sister tried to attack me after my neighbor tried to seduce me. On top of having to marry Zeus and my grandmother despising me, life wasn't great at the moment.

She turned and went towards her room. "Now, I've got to get ready because we have to go taste cakes today."

"Thank you. For helping. I'm sorry I didn't think you would."

Persephone smiled and walked back over and kissed my forehead. "Don't worry dear, I understand. I haven't been the best mother to you, but I'm trying my best for you not to have to deal with some of the same shit I've had to deal with. Just have faith in that human of yours."

And I did, because Huntley was the best thing that had ever happened to me.

Chapter 14

HUNTLEY

I glared over the table at A.J., who stared out the window, tied to a chair, ignoring my gaze. It had been an entire day now and he was still in the flat for some reason. He had told us how sorry he was about hurting Chrys and that it wasn't supposed to turn out the way it did, but that was complete bullshit. There had to be more to why he was here—he surely had alternative motives. There was no way that he would finally decide he had a conscious after what he did.

None of us trusted him, which was half the reason he was still here. We didn't want him to go report anything to anyone. We hadn't given him any details about our plan or anything, but we still feared he might have been watching us this whole time and that was why he was in London, especially since his story wasn't making sense.

For all we knew, he was just about to report to Zeus when I spotted him, collecting information so that Zeus knew exactly what we were up to. Question was, how much had he already told Zeus?

"You can stop staring at me Huntley, it's starting to get on my nerves," A.J. commented.

I shook my head and clenched my fist. "No, I'm just going to keep staring. I don't trust you and don't want you to have an opportunity to start shit again."

"Like you are smart enough to catch anything."

I stood up, slamming my hands on the table.

Pothos gave me a reproachful look. "Don't damage my table, please!"

A.J. rolled his eyes. "Always with the anger Huntley, you would think you would give it a rest by now."

It was hard to hold in all the anger and took everything to not further break the table. "And you would think you would give it a rest when it came down to being a complete dick and yet here you are!"

He shook his head but didn't answer. He knew I

had a point. A.J. should be killed for what he did, but he can't die, unless Chrys killed him. Zeus promised him immortality, although Chrys had the ability to kill anything, or bring anything back to life. Including me.

"We can't monitor him constantly though," Prometheus commented. "So we need to decide what we will do with him. He might know too much, but we can't kill him."

"We could always torture him, tie him up, and see if he will give us more information," Mel smiled. I liked her more and more with each passing day. But also feared her more and more each day.

"No, at least not yet," Prometheus said as he rubbed her back. "We need him on our side. He might be beneficial."

"Scaring him will get him on our side," Pothos added. "That's how Zeus works."

"He has a point," I added. "I mean, I'm up for torturing and giving him a little motivation to tell us the truth."

"It won't do you any good, I'm immortal and besides, I am telling the truth."

"Just because you are immortal doesn't mean you can't be tortured, believe me," Prometheus smiled. "I can tell you horror stories of the things Zeus has made me do. I also can tell you experiences of others. All of them have given me ideas of what to do to you. And believe me, there is a lengthy list to choose from."

"Oh, I like that idea. Can I be the first one to have at it? I think I deserve it."

A.J. looked nervous but went on. "I'm not lying, I am not helping Zeus in anything and want to help Chrys."

"What about Poseidon? Are you helping him with anything?" Pothos asked.

A.J. hesitated and glanced back and forth between us. Yeah, he was totally hiding something. He may not be working for Zeus, but he was definitely helping his father.

Pothos smiled. "You are, but what? I haven't heard of Poseidon doing anything worth our attention, and the seas have been rather calm, as if he is focusing on something. What is it?"

A.J. looked out the window, as if contemplating what to tell us. So we were right, he was up to something. He was just a big son of a bitch.

"He… he is mad about what happened and doesn't think Chrys should live. He is hoping that you guys will get her out of there and then when you do, he wants to make his move."

We all stared at him. Seriously, he was betraying her again? And in this time for her life? What kind of douche did you have to be to betray your friend twice?

I was the first to go over and punch him straight in the face. "You fucking asshole! You were just going to use her again! How could you fucking even think about doing that? God!"

He spat out some bloody spit. "I said I'm sorry! He forced me to! Poseidon found me and demanded I help him, or else he would tie me to a boulder in the middle of the northern ocean! I would just be drowning for centuries! I don't know about you, but I don't want to go through that!"

"Oh, I bet I can think of tortures worse than Poseidon even can dream about. Just try me." Prometheus stood up and grabbed A.J. by the back of the neck. "Now, what did Poseidon say?"

Fear filled A.J.'s eyes, unlike I had seen in his before. He knew that Prometheus wasn't kidding around, and that drowning in the sea for centuries was just the tip of the iceberg for what Prometheus had planned.

"H-he has his men watching you. He doesn't care if Zeus gets screwed over, but just wants Chrys to be dead."

"So he knows of our plans?"

A.J. quickly nodded. "Yes."

"And wants us to succeed so he can ambush us as we leave and kill her?" Prometheus clarified.

A.J. nodded again. "Yes."

Prometheus laughed as he paced around A.J. "Fucking Poseidon, thinking he can do whatever he wants. He has such an ego." Letting out a sigh, he bent down so his eyes were at the same level as A.J.'s. A.J.'s eyes widened even more.

"And how does he plan on killing Chrys?" Prometheus asked. "Other than with Zeus' lightning, there isn't anyone powerful enough to stop her."

A.J. squeaked. "I don't remember."

Prometheus picked A.J. up by the back of his neck and dragged him and the chair he was tied to over to the kitchen. "Okay, fine, we will do this the hard way."

"No wait! I'll tell you!" A.J. screamed as Poseidon pulled out the ice pick from the knife block.

"Too late." Prometheus smiled, his teeth almost looking shark-like. With that smile, he would make a great villain. I had to look away and not throw up as Prometheus stabbed A.J. straight in the left eye with the pick. A.J. let out a most horrific scream. You see this kind of shit in movies, but when you saw it in real life, it was completely different. This was something that I would never forget.

I wondered if anyone in the surrounding buildings would call the cops, and how we would explain A.J.'s state of torture. I just prayed they ignored the screams like most humans did.

Prometheus didn't hesitate as he pulled the pick out, which made a disgusting flesh ripping sound, and stabbed A.J. in the other eye. I honestly didn't think Prometheus would be this brutal, but didn't feel any sympathy for A.J.. He had lied again and again and his deceit caused Chrys to marry Zeus. He had been planning it for centuries—looking Chrys straight in the face as he lied to her and plotted to use her to get out of the Underworld. I didn't even understand why he would want to leave the paradise that Hades had offered to come back to this world. This world sucked.

Glancing over at Prometheus, I found his eyes to be ice cold. I knew these gods were scary, but watching one use a weapon instead of their power was rather terrifying. He had never been this forceful with anyone else, although I supposed that was because A.J. was more human than he was god. He was strong, but not strong enough to go up against a god, or I guess titan, in Prometheus' case.

Prometheus wiped off the blood and gross bits that covered the ice pick. "Now while you heal from that, which should only take an hour, two hours tops, I want you to think about what you will tell us about Poseidon."

A.J. whimpered as his head draped down, blood pouring down onto his shirt. Prometheus turned to face us with a brief smile.

"Who wants to watch Doctor Who while we wait?" Prometheus asked.

We all went over to the couch and sat down, not saying a word. Even Mel was silent but wrapped herself around Prometheus. It had been a sight to see, but I had a feeling these gods were used to this sort of thing by now. That, and Mel could really bring you nightmares.

As the episode of Doctor Who started, one of my favorites featuring the underrated 9th Doctor witnessing the end of the world, the doorbell rang. My heart felt as if it had skipped a beat. Was it Poseidon? Was it one of his minions? Or had Aphrodite gotten the message to Hera and she had decided to come down here herself?

Or was it the cops because someone reported the screaming?

Pothos quickly got the door and a woman with smooth tanned skin, braided amber hair, wearing an all-white suit, stood in the entry way. The cut on the suit was rather low and I had to look away. She also wore tall white heels, which begged the question of how she managed to walk without toppling over.

Was this Hera?

Pothos, Melinoe, and Prometheus all bowed. I followed what they did, now assuming this was in fact Hera.

She gestured to them. "You may rise."

We all got up and she appeared as if she was sizing each of us up. "Aphrodite said you all wanted to speak with me."

Prometheus nodded. "Yes, it is about this wedding."

She let out a little laugh, as if he she found it amusing. A.J. let out an audible moan as he still laid on the floor in pain. She glanced over at him in the kitchen, but turned back to us as if a man with his eyes stabbed out was something normal to see. "What about it?"

"We have a way to stop it, but need your help," Prometheus explained.

She stepped forward and sat down on the couch. "Let me explain a little something to you all. Zeus and I have had a lot of disputes lately, mainly just getting old and worn out with each other. When he came back to Olympus to tell me he found a new wife, you want to know what my response was?"

We all stared at her, waiting for her to say.

"I was ecstatic. Finally, someone to get him the hell away from me!"

I did not like how she said that. Was she saying she wanted this marriage to happen? All the stories showed how jealous she was when Zeus went after someone else.

I glanced over at Prometheus, who seemed as confused as I was.

Prometheus asked. "I beg your pardon?"

Hera stood up. "I want Zeus to marry the daughter of Hades, and then I will be free of his crap."

"Then why are you here?" Prometheus asked.

"To stop you."

Chapter 15

CHRYS

I was excited to taste the cakes. I loved sweets, and at least it would pass the time while waiting for the others to come and stop the wedding. Nothing could corrupt something as innocent as cake tasting.

My mouth watered at the thought. I wondered what flavors they had. Chocolate? Vanilla? Red velvet? Champagne? There were so many choices and I couldn't wait to try every one. Then I would make notes for what kind of cake I would serve at Huntley and I's wedding.

I blushed at the thought. I couldn't wait to run away with Huntley and marry him. And be with him.

And see if my father beats him into a pulp or not.

I think at this point that father didn't care if I married Huntley and would prefer it. It was him or Zeus, and anything was better than Zeus.

Well, almost anything. I think if I had to choose between Poseidon and Zeus, I would pick Zeus. Poseidon seemed to be more of a pervert.

Then there was Apollo…

I shook my head, trying to forget all of them and just focus on Huntley. He was what kept me going, the person I cared about the most. He was there for me, making sure I was safe. I should have listened to him. He warned me about going to the mortal realm, and I didn't listen. I just followed my rage and did as A.J. said. And then was tricked. And then ended up in this engagement.

We reached the cake shop and there in front of the entrance stood Zeus. I froze in my tracks. I didn't expect him to be here and realized I hadn't seen him since that day over a year ago. My heart raced, and I felt horror sweep over me.

What if Huntley and the others didn't succeed? What if I wasn't saved from this eternal torture?

He walked up to me and grabbed my hand and kissed it. "You look fetching today, Chrys."

I opened my mouth, but nothing came out. I didn't expect to see him like this, I didn't know what to do.

"She had an interminable night and is a bit out of it," Persephone said.

He turned to her and smiled. "I hope there was no trouble."

My heart was beating even louder. Oh shit, was he going to find out about how I tried to escape? If he did, was he going to kill me?

"No, just Apollo and his usual shit. Sometimes he can be loud."

I let out the breath I was holding. That was a close one.

"Ah yes. Just pay him no mind. He is just a lonely wolf with too much time on his hands."

I nodded and tried to fake a smile but couldn't.

After me not responding for a moment, Zeus turned to the cake shop. "Shall we begin?"

"Yeah," I mustered up the courage to speak. "Let's."

We took a seat inside the café. It was filled with photos of cake designs with the different gods this shop had served over the years. I didn't know why they wanted to post all the pictures, as I believed this was the only cake place in all of Olympus. Did they have to prove something?

"Oh Zeus." The pink-skinned nymph ran over. "I

feel so honored that you have joined us today to try the cakes."

"Well, you sell the most delicious cakes in all of Olympus."

My mother kicked me as she saw my mouth open. I didn't know how she knew I would make a sarcastic comment.

"Yes, your cakes are the most delicious in all the kingdom. I am glad I could bring my daughter here to try them."

The nymph gave my mother a look. "Oh, Persephone, I can't remember, what kind of cake did you get for your wedding again?"

Mother let out a sigh. "Yes, I know. Hades' chefs made one, not you."

"Oh, that's right. I keep forgetting."

I held back a laugh. Was she mad at my mother for not having her make her cake? She got married in the Underworld, so the cooks there made everything. It seemed as if everyone made comments about it.

I couldn't see why my mother just detoured the conversation. It had been centuries and she was still dealing with this crap.

The nymph turned back to Zeus. "I'll get some of your favorites ready. I will be right back." With that, she skipped to the kitchen. Now it was just the three of us.

Zeus grabbed my hand and traced it. "I hope that picking out the wedding dress yesterday went well."

I didn't know what to say, because honestly, I hated the dress. I glanced over at my mom. She put on one of her fake smiles. "Yeah, it went smoothly."

"That is good." Zeus picked up my hand and kissed it. "I can't wait to see it." He bent forward and whispered in my ear. "And take it off"

I froze. This was not something I wanted to hear. I felt like running away at that moment as fast as I could, but it would be for nothing. Hermes had taken back his key card and I was left with no way of getting out of here.

But Huntley and the others had a plan—we would find a way out of this. And if not, maybe I would just bolt on my wedding day. Yeah, that sounded perfect. At that moment, I didn't think I would care if I died or not. I just wanted out of here.

The nymph brought out a plate full of fresh slices of cake, each with a little label. There had to be a dozen unique flavors. If the fact Zeus wasn't sitting next to me, his hand now tracing the inside of my thigh, I would be ecstatic. Instead, however, I wanted to throw up.

I tried each one of them, though, and they were all very good. I could see why it was the only cake shop in all of Olympus, although I had a feeling if anyone tried to open up a shop, this nymph would just murder them.

After taking a bite of the last one, I leaned back, stuffed.

Zeus patted my leg, making me jump. "Now, what do you think of these cakes, my sweet flower?"

I did not like that he called me his flower. Only my father called me that, and it made me cringe every time he said it. If Hades heard him call me his flower, I had a feeling he would stab him right then and there. I know I wanted to.

I shook my head. "I really don't care, they all were fantastic." And they were, if I hadn't felt like barfing every moment of today.

He tapped his chin. "Hmm, well what about the chocolate one? Chocolate is always good."

I shrugged. "Sure."

"But which filling with the chocolate? With cherries, raspberries, or pomegranates?" Zeus asked.

I turned to him. "Pomegranates?"

He saw the look in my eyes and laughed. "Yeah, I suppose that would be ironic with where you are from. I am not talking about pomegranates from the Underworld though, just ones from Earth. I'm not going to drug anyone, not like your father."

I ignored his comment about my father drugging anyone and saw my mother watching me, as if she was confused about my comment. Neither she nor father had ever talked about the pomegranates they had consumed. I technically shouldn't have known about that, except Huntley had found them a few years back and we had been sneaking them every once in a while.

I said nothing as Zeus talked to the owner of the bakery and ordered the wedding cake. I wondered what size it would be, considering a lot of the gods were coming. He was Zeus after all. It wasn't like a wedding, especially one as controversial as this, happened often.

He ordered all three different types of chocolate cakes, and it sounded like the bride and groom's cake would be the pomegranate chocolate cake. At least that tasted good, but I kind of wished the pomegranates in it were the ones from the Underworld. Then maybe I could get through all of this if it didn't go according to Huntley's plan.

Maybe next time I was in the Underworld I would steal enough to keep me in that state for three months.

As we stepped outside, Hermes was standing there. He looked nervous, as if he had something important to say.

"What is it?" Zeus asked.

Hermes pulled Zeus to the side and told him something. Zeus' face got serious for a moment, then smiled as he looked over at me.

"It's fine then, she will take care of the issue and I won't have to worry anymore."

Hermes nodded and Zeus came back over. "Well, I have to run as I have a lot to do." He kissed my cheek. "Soon, my sweet flower."

I shivered as he turned and left towards the central palace. I let out a breath I didn't realize I was holding this entire time and gave Hermes a confused look.

"What was that all about?" I asked.

He hesitated for a moment. "I shouldn't tell you. He would be furious with me if I did."

My heart quickened. "What is it?"

Hermes let out a slight sigh. "Hera… she went down to the mortal realm to take care of what she found to be a threat to this wedding."

"What do you mean?"

Hermes glanced around. "How about we go back to Persephone's place? I don't want anyone to overhear."

My hands were shaking as we ventured towards my mother's apartment. No one paid us mind as we made our way through the city and back towards where the apartments were. After we went inside, Hermes closed the door behind us.

"Aphrodite told Hera about Huntley and the others in hopes she would help them get in since she gets jealous of other women and Zeus…"

Hermes went on. "Apparently this time she is sick of his antics and wants out of the marriage. She went down to stop Huntley and the others, not to help them. Zeus won't do anything because, well, he doesn't want this wedding stopped either."

It felt like my heart had dropped into my stomach. "What… what is she going to do?"

Hermes shrugged. "I don't know, but with her it is never good."

Huntley was in danger. "I have to go to him, she will kill him. I can't let her hurt him!"

Hermes grabbed my arm. "You can't leave here. If you do, then Zeus will kill us both. You understand? Huntley wouldn't want that, now would he?"

"No, but if he's dead, he wouldn't care either way."

"If he's dead, you would just see him in the Underworld, wouldn't you?" Hermes asked. "I don't see the problem of that."

He had a point. The problem was, he couldn't do anything to help me get out of this if he were in the Underworld. No one was allowed to leave. Well, usually.

"We don't know if she would kill him. She might do something else, like turn him into a plant or something," Persephone explained.

My eyes widened. "That would be horrible! That can't happen! Please, Hermes, let me go down there!"

Hermes shook his head. "I can't."

"Then I will," Persephone said. "I will go stop her."

I couldn't believe what I was hearing. Was my mother helping me with all this? It seemed impossible, but here she was, doing just that.

Hermes shook his head again. "No, if Zeus found out then he would know I told you. Besides, you aren't allowed to leave during these two weeks either. There have been rumors that you were helping Huntley and his gang."

I couldn't believe what I was hearing. There was no way to help Huntley and if he was cursed like my mom said, I might not be able to bring him back.

This was complete shit.

"But I mean, I am the messenger of Zeus, and Hera is still technically his wife. It is my duty to make sure none of those gods that are helping Huntley hurt her. And I guess if stopping her is the only way to keep her safe. I guess it would be my duty," Hermes gave me a little wink.

He would help me. I didn't quite understand why, exactly, wasn't he working for Zeus? Wasn't he in charge of making sure I didn't stop this wedding? "What?"

"I'm helping you. But if you tell a soul, I will take Huntley to the Underworld myself, do I make myself clear?"

I nodded. "Yes, now please hurry!"

Hermes hurried out the door. I looked over at my mother. She was looking out the window.

"What is it?" I asked.

She nodded out towards the beach. Apollo was standing there, his arms folded with a slight smirk. "He has been watching for a bit. I think he's been eavesdropping too. I'm not sure how much he knows or has picked up."

It was just one stress after another. "What should we do about him?" I asked.

She shrugged. "Not sure if there is anything we can do. We will just wait to see if he makes a move. He won't go straight to Zeus with anything, he will try to get something for the information he has. He might have nothing and is just playing with us. God, I hate him."

I glanced back out the door and I could tell his smirk grew a little. He knows we were talking about him. Did he have dog-like hearing or something? It was possible since he could transform into a wolf then he might be able to hear like them. I could see why my mom had a hatred for him. He seemed to be trouble just waiting to happen.

Hopefully he was bluffing, and I wouldn't have to deal with his shit. I swore if he caused a problem on top of my many other problems, I would snap and take him out with me.

Chapter 16

HUNTLEY

Well crap. This shit again.

I wondered why nothing ever went according to plan. It was the most frustrating thing ever; I was finding out. Why couldn't any of this just ever work? Gods made everything complicated, I could see why the stories were all so messed up—these guys just got in each other's way.

I couldn't wait until it was all over. As long as I survived. Chrys and I would just stay in the Underworld forever, where it was safe and peaceful. Man, did I long for those days.

Fucking A.J. and his fucking plan to betray Chrys.

Hera stood there, in her low-cut white suit, ready to destroy us all, or curse us all, I wasn't sure which.

She smiled at all of us, as if pondering what to do with us. I had a feeling none of them were going to be fun.

I heard a whimper to the side of me and found A.J. was coming to after all the pain he had endured. I wondered if she would hurt him. She didn't know level of his involvement, nor did I think she cared. She just wanted to get rid of all of us once and for all.

It made little sense, though, as in most of the stories, Hera got jealous and wanted to stop her cheating husband. I guess she had a breaking point. I couldn't blame her—I had seen women leave men for far less.

The energy of the room shifted as she gathered up energy.

"Wait!" I called out.

Hera gave me a look, as if a pathetic human couldn't stop her, but I felt the energy slowing down. "Do you think you can stop me human?"

"I think you should wait and hear what I have to say."

She laughed. "As if what a human has to say could ever affect what I have already decided."

"Will you at least hear me out?" I asked.

She looked me over, as if I was some kind of

intriguing pest. "Fine, I'll hear what you have to say, only because I am curious."

Here was my chance. "I love her, okay? Chrys is the most amazing person I have ever met. She cared for me when no one else would. She has so much she could be capable of in the Underworld helping her father. If you help us, we will just go back to there and no one will ever have to see us again. She will be out of your hair. And you can just leave Zeus and do what you want, no one is asking you to stay with him. I doubt it would be long until Zeus finds some other women that he wants to sleep with. Just wait until then and let us help Chrys. She doesn't deserve this."

Hera was silent for a moment, then took a few steps towards me. "You love her, don't you human?"

I nodded. "Yes, I do."

She traced her finger along my cheek. "You stupid, stupid human. You know what happens when a human falls in love with a god?"

"What?" I asked.

She removed her hand and then held it up. "They end up being cursed!"

Shit. She didn't listen. I turned to run and get the hell out of there as the energy grew and her eyes turned white as she summoned all her power. This couldn't be the end, it just couldn't. I didn't want to be turned into a frog for all eternity, or worse. I wasn't sure what could be worse than that, but I wasn't about to find out.

Suddenly, before Hera could use the power she accumulated, Prometheus jumped towards her as he reached for something in his pocket. He pulled out a vial that Hades had given me and put a drop on his finger. He quickly, before Hera could react, placed his finger in her mouth and she passed out.

What the fuck?

Everything was quiet for a moment as if we were all just trying to figure out what had just happened, and what Prometheus just did. Pothos, Mel, and I were all across the room, trying to escape whatever would happen. Prometheus was standing over Hera's now unconscious body, taking a deep breath as if he wasn't sure if his plan would work. A.J. was still in the kitchen, moaning.

"What just happened?" I asked.

Prometheus bent down and searched for Hera's pulse. "She is fine, it's just the River Lethe drop that knocked her out. Made of Henbane extract, actually, not that you know what that means. She will have a momentary lapse of memory. I'm not sure how much she will forget, though. Hopefully just what happened here, and not more."

I rubbed my face. Great, she might have forgotten who she was. That would suck. Would Zeus find out what we did? Would he kill us for it? Would he even care at this point? "Okay. So we just will have to deal with that when she wakes up. I guess it's better than her killing us all."

"Yup…" Prometheus sighed as he examined Hera. "Someone want to help me get her onto the couch? I don't think she will appreciate waking up on the floor."

Pothos and I helped him lift her up. She seemed to weigh more than she looked, probably because she looked like she was pure muscle. I guess most goddesses were like this, as all of them were badasses.

Prometheus clapped his hands together. "There, now we just have to get our story right for when she wakes—"

The door crashed open and Hermes came barging in, almost singing. "Stand back everyone, nothing here to see! Just imminent danger and in the middle of it, me! Yes, Hermes is here, hair blowing in the breeze! The day needs my saving—" he glanced around and saw us just simple staring at him. "Oh, there's nothing going on…"

"You are, like, two minutes too late." Pothos explained. "But I really appreciate the song. It would have been cool. The kicking down my door wasn't cool, though."

Hermes ignored the comment about the door. "I've been wanting to use it for years and never had the chance. To be honest, I'm kind of bummed I didn't get to use it just now."

Pothos placed his hand on Hermes' shoulder. "One day. One day."

Hermes nodded in agreement, then he glanced over. "So, what did I miss?"

Prometheus sighed. "Well, Hera showed up and tried to kill us, but I used a drop of River Lethe to knock her out. Now we are just waiting for her to come around so we can figure out how much she remembers."

He glanced in the kitchen and nodded. "And that?"

Prometheus didn't miss a beat. "That's A.J.. I stabbed him in the eyes with an ice pick. He's been causing us trouble"

Hermes nodded. "Makes sense."

"Why are you here, Hermes?" Prometheus asked as he sat down. "You aren't exactly on our trust list. You serve Zeus, after all."

"Ah, yes. I came to stop Hera from attacking you all in case she might get hurt. Who knows what you lot are capable of. Also, because Chrys wanted me to make sure Huntley was fine. She said nothing about the rest of you so I just assumed you all could die or whatnot."

Mel stuck her tongue out at him and Pothos shook his head. Hermes laughed and saw me staring at him, trying to figure out what his game was.

"You helped Chrys?" I asked.

He nodded. "Yeah, she seems to like you for some odd reason. Not sure why. You are just a human. However, all the gods seem to fall for you humans. It makes no sense."

Pothos held his hand and sarcastically commented. "True love doesn't matter if it is god or human, as long as they get banged."

Pothos and Hermes laughed, but I just rolled my eyes. All we needed was another sarcastic god in our midst. I guess when you had so much time on your hands, you had to deal with it somehow. "What did Chrys say?"

Hermes shrugged. "She just wanted me to make sure you were alright, especially since you lot are the ones trying to stop her from marrying Zeus. She found out Hera was coming here and freaked out. If

I didn't stop her, she would have risked her life to come down."

Prometheus raised an eyebrow. "And how did she find out about Hera?"

Hermes smiled. "I don't know. Some god must have told her."

"Mhmm."

"And you decided to help us?" I asked.

Hermes shrugged again. "I helped you before. What, did you think that was just a onetime thing?"

"What do you mean you have helped us before?" Pothos asked.

"Oh, Huntley didn't tell you? I caught him in the Underworld in Hades' office. I know what you will attempt, and to be honest I'm not sure it will work. Hopefully, but you have to consider Zeus doesn't follow any rules."

"It's the only thing we have. It will work." Prometheus rubbed his head. "Now, what are we going to do with you?"

Hermes raised an eyebrow. "What do you mean?"

"I don't trust you," Prometheus said. "Especially since you are Zeus' righthand man."

"I know you have the stuff used for a marriage in the Underworld. I know you will use it to declare Chrys married and that under the laws of the

Underworld that she can't marry someone else. You are going to make a deal with Zeus that you will monitor her and will obey his every whim. Am I wrong?"

None of us said anything. He was, in fact, correct.

"And what are you going to do with that information?" Prometheus asked.

"Get you into Olympus, of course."

Prometheus narrowed his eyes. "But why help us?"

Hermes paused for a moment, as if trying to explain. Prometheus wasn't being very trusting, which I guess when you had dealt with Zeus for so long, it made sense. "Because Chrys doesn't deserve to marry Zeus. He is an abusive asshole, worse than all the other gods put together. I can't imagine what he would do with her, especially since she is the daughter of Hades. He loves to torment Hades." Hermes smiles. "And because then I won't have to go to the Underworld twice a year. It's a pain, and Hades and I don't get along very well."

Everyone was quiet, wondering if he was telling the truth. Hermes had seen me sneak into the Underworld and hadn't told Zeus about it. That was weeks ago and he had the time to betray us. Why would he change now? He had enough information to have Zeus kill us.

"I think he is telling the truth," I said. "He saw me and Hades talking with the box. He knew what we were doing and reported nothing. If he was going to stop us, he would have done it sooner."

Prometheus was silent for a moment, mulling things over. "I suppose we can trust him. We need help figuring out what to do with Hera. It would only be with him we could get anything to work from here on out."

"And I have a plan," Hermes explained. "I'm just not sure what you want to do with him." He nodded towards A.J.. "I think stabbing him in the eyes will make him tell on us and that you should keep a watchful eye on him. No pun intended."

"He knows he deserved his punishment. But we will also need to deal with the information he gave to Poseidon. Seems he is trying to set up a trap for when our plan succeeds. Poseidon has been wanting to get revenge on Chrys."

"So you need me to check on Poseidon. I can have that be arranged. Poseidon isn't as strong as he thinks he is."

Prometheus nodded. "That would be very helpful, yes. Now for what we will do when Hera wakes up, what do you have in mind?"

Hermes smiled. "It's very simple, just bear with me."

Chapter 17

CHRYS

I bit at my nail. This was torture, waiting for Hermes to come back. I had no idea if Huntley was okay or not, and I hated waiting and not knowing. Would Hermes come straight here and tell me it was all fine? Would he lie if something did happen? Did he actually go down to save them? There were too many scenarios running through my head that I couldn't focus.

"You and Huntley do the same things when you are worried. It is quite interesting," mother commented as she sat and watched me pace.

"Don't most people pace?" I asked.

"Yeah, but there's a certain energy about you. And you both are very impatient. Huntley paces so much he wore the carpet where he walks. Pothos is pretty pissed about it."

That made me laugh a little. Huntley sure couldn't keep still. That was one of the things I liked about him. We both would just keep going if no one stopped us.

"I guess that is why we get along, because we are a lot alike, or at least share a lot of the same attributes."

Persephone smiled gently. "Yeah, I can see that. Except I don't think Huntley could handle a lot of the tasks you do for your father. I don't think he could rule over the Underworld."

"Who knows if I will ever rule. It's not like father will retire ever and he is one of the original gods, son of Kronos. Nothing can stop him."

Mother kept smiling but said nothing. Did she think father would give his throne to me? Was there something she wasn't telling me?

I changed the topic. "Why did you decide to help Huntley?"

She looked at me like that was some kind of insulting question. "Do I need a reason to help my daughter?"

I tried to pick my words carefully, knowing it would end up just being another fight. "No offense mother, but you and I haven't been on speaking terms for a while. It's not like you have shown me you wanted to help."

She let out a sigh. "That is different and has a lot to do with stuff you don't understand. I wouldn't ever want you to get into a marriage with someone you didn't love, let alone Zeus."

"Like you and father? It's apparent that you didn't love each other, or at least you don't love him. Are the stories true? Did he kidnap you to make you marry him? Knowing father, I find that hard to believe, but I'm not sure what else could have happened."

Her eyes saddened. "It was a long time ago, and I loved your father, but things change after centuries. People change."

I crossed my arms. "I don't believe father has ever changed, and that is why most of Olympus hates him. He doesn't conform to anybody's ideas of him or what he does."

"You are right, he never changed. That was one of the problems."

I shook my head. "I don't understand, if he never changed, he is still the man you fell in love with. Why would you not love him anymore then?"

Persephone stood up and peered out the window.

"I have never stopped loving your father. Hades means everything to me, and I hate being away from him."

I let out a sharp laugh. "What the hell are you talking about? You verbally say you don't want to be in the Underworld and that you hate it. Constantly! Nothing you have ever done in the past centuries I have been alive has shown me you have one ounce of love for Hades. So don't tell me this lie."

She turned to me. "You don't understand, Chrys, you do not know the hell I have gone through to be with him. It's hard not to act out, to not find something to make the pain go away! I constantly hear how everyone hates him, how I am just his trophy he stole! That people think I was kidnapped and raped when that was never the story. I have been told so many versions of my story that I don't even remember what happened anymore.

"Everyone keeps making him out to be the evil guy and sometimes I believe them. I don't know who is right nor who is wrong and I just want the voices to stop. I play up the bitch woman who hates her husband act up here so people will just leave me the hell alone. Then the centuries went by and that fake person became the real me. I have done all the drugs, slept with loads of men, just trying to get the pain to go away."

I stared at her. I never heard her side in all this. What would I have done if people told me that my husband was the villain so often that I didn't know what was the truth? What if everyone hated someone I loved and no matter what I said, they wouldn't change their minds about him? What would I have done in a similar situation?

"And you know what the worst part of it all was?" She asked with tears in her eyes.

I shook my head, now feeling sad that I brought it up. This seemed like something she was struggling with for a long time. I wished she could have said something earlier. Father would have understood.

Maybe he understood. Maybe that was why he let her do all the things she did. That was until I screwed up. Now I felt guilty. This truly was all my fault and I couldn't blame anyone else.

Well, maybe A.J..

Mother went on. "He got to keep you all this time. I never got to take you, to show the others the love Hades had for me. I could never talk about my dear daughter and how much I cared for her. I had to leave her behind every time I left, and it broke my heart."

I didn't know what to say. I never thought about what it must have been like, especially when I was younger and growing up, to have to leave your child behind and not mention her to a soul. They had kept me a secret for centuries from everyone. And she kept that secret so I would never get hurt.

Tears ran down my face. "I'm sorry. This is all my fault. If I just stayed in the Underworld, I wouldn't have put us all in danger. I have everything coming, I deserve this."

She shook her head. "It isn't your fault. This was so long in the making that it is possible it will never be fixed. I just wanted you to know, none of this is your fault. It's just the stupid world we live in. And some day, my Flower, you will change it. You will bring an end to this nonsense. You have to."

I didn't believe I was strong enough to fulfill this prophecy. I didn't think I could ever take down Zeus or Olympus. Yet, that belief got me in this mess in the first place. Zeus was the only one who could kill me, or could stop me from hurting any other god. That was why he wanted me close—to make sure I didn't cause trouble for him. If I did, he would kill me that instant.

"I don't think I can, mother. I don't even know if I will be able to get out of this marriage, let alone take down Zeus."

She held me tight and stroked my head as both of us had tears coming down our eyes. "You can, Flower, I really think you are meant to. I wish we had told you sooner, but we were too scared. Now you can see why."

I let out a brief snort of a laugh. "Yeah, I see why."

"Your father and I will keep you safe. And you have Huntley figuring something out. He is a keeper, that one. I wasn't sure when he first showed up in the Underworld if he would be a suitable fit, but these past few months he has gone up against gods. Not many mortals would do that."

I laughed. "Yeah, he is perfect. I still can't believe I talked father into letting him be a tutor."

She laughed a little. "Yeah, there is no way he believed Huntley could tutor you in anything. But he saw that you wanted a friend. It took a lot of persuading on my part, and I don't think he ever trusted Huntley until now."

I didn't know my mother had spoken to father about Huntley to get him to be a tutor. Maybe she was more observant than I thought, since I did really need a friend. The only person I had to hang out with was A.J..

The thought of him made my blood boil.

"Then there is fucking A.J.. I can't believe he betrayed me like he did."

"If I ever see that boy again, I will smash him into dust."

I gave her a smirk. "Not before I do, mother. I will show him what happens when you betray a friend, especially one who is a daughter of Hades."

"No, one who is a daughter of Persephone. Believe me, I have shown some men their place. And have kicked more asses than your father."

I let out a chuckle. I could see that, especially after seeing her hit Apollo in the head with a magazine. It surprised me that's all it took for him to back down, but he might have just known what my mother was really capable of.

Now coming back to what was going on around me, I remembered what I was worried about: Huntley and if he would make it out of this in one piece. I mean, he was already dead, but I didn't want him cursed or worse.

I let out a sigh. "Do you think Huntley's plan will work?"

Mother nodded. "Yes, your father and I came up with it before I left. There are certain laws in the Underworld that even Olympus has to follow. Ones that have to do with marriage."

I looked at her, confused. "What do you mean?"

"We will fake a wedding between you and Prometheus. He is the only one we can trust, and Zeus won't question a titan like him. Zeus had tortured him previously, so Zeus wouldn't believe he would try to trick him again."

I wasn't sure how I felt about this news, as that meant I would trade marrying Zeus for marrying someone else I didn't even know. Although Prometheus was a little more attractive than Zeus, and the whole situation a lot less gross, I still didn't love him. "I would have to marry him?"

She shook her head. "No, you would just act like you married him. We will take pictures of the ceremony and show Zeus."

"Why couldn't we have done this earlier?" I asked. "Wouldn't that have made sense?"

She shook her head. "Prometheus wouldn't have been able to get into the Underworld and you wouldn't have been able to go to the mortal realm without Hermes reporting on you. I know we are cutting it close, but we have no choice. Getting him up here is the only way to do it and stop the wedding."

So that was their plan? It didn't sound like it was thought through that well. I worried it would fail now. "Isn't Zeus going to be completely pissed that we did that right before his wedding?" I asked. "I mean, I don't see how this will solve anything."

"Prometheus is older than Zeus and although Zeus is more powerful, he will listen to Prometheus. Prometheus will convince him he will watch over you, and if there is anything wrong, that he will report immediately to Zeus. You will probably be watched for quite a while, but after they start to trust you, then you two can move apart and you can go back to your own life in the Underworld."

This plan sucked more and more as I learned about it. "How long will that take?"

Mother shrugged. "As long as it needs. But you won't have to marry Zeus and Prometheus will take care of you a lot better than Zeus ever would."

Was this better? Would it actually go according to plan? I couldn't believe that Huntley would go with this, as it still meant I would have to be with someone else for a while. He had been with Prometheus this whole time, so I guess I could trust him. Prometheus tried to save me after all. He couldn't be the bad guy in all this.

Only time would tell.

Chapter 18

HUNTLEY

This plan was so going to fail.

I looked up out of Hermes' courier bag. Yeah, that's right. We were somehow shrunken, like that one movie, and were hanging out in his bag. I didn't quite understand how it worked, because, well; I was human and had never been shrunken by magic before. But somehow, two hours after Hermes arrived, we were in his courier bag.

When did my life take such a weird turn?

Thank god it didn't smell. If he left some week-old egg salad sandwich in here, I would have been pissed. Instead, it was a rather clean pack, with some papers, pencils, and pens, which were all enormous now. They looked like those fake ones you could buy as a joke. I always wanted to show up to class with one of those, except I didn't go to class, and no one would have thought it was funny. I made a note to find one later and show Chrys. She would think it was funny.

Prometheus, Pothos, Mel, and A.J. were all with me. We were still in the apartment, waiting for Hera to wake up. Once she did, Hermes would convince her she cursed us all and help her go back to Olympus. Hermes would then take us to Persephone and we could start the second part of the plan, which was marrying Chrys to Prometheus.

We questioned Hermes further as to why Hera would have wanted to stop us instead of wanting to stop Chrys. He didn't go into too much detail, but it seemed that Zeus had become a bigger pig and asshole in these last few centuries. He treated her like just an object and didn't care that she was putting all the time into their relationship and he was just going after other goddesses or humans if she wouldn't satisfy him. I couldn't imagine what he would do to Chrys, which made this mission even more critical.

A.J. moaned and rolled around on the bottom of the carrier bag. His eyes were almost healed, but he still was clearly in pain. Also, it was gross to watch them heal back the way they were, and I tried to ignore him. I didn't feel pity for him, though, as he deserved far worse, but we couldn't leave him behind. We didn't need him telling Prometheus anything else, as we didn't even know what Prometheus knew in the first place.

It felt like an hour had gone by since Hermes shrank us and put in the bag. I hated being compacted like this and wanted to pace, but couldn't for a handful of reasons. One, because there wasn't room and I would run into someone else, which they yelled at me earlier about. Two, because I might knock over the pencils or pens and have them crush us, again. They also yelled at me for that. So, they made me stay still. I bit at my loose hang nail.

"Hera, wake up." I could hear Hermes say. "Rise and shine, beautiful queen."

I heard her moan as she was trying to come to. "Where am I?"

"Don't you remember, you came to prevent that human and Prometheus from stopping the wedding?"

"Oh, that's right. Ugh, what happened? Why was I asleep?"

Hermes answered. "You used up a lot of power

turning them into flies, see?"

I had been the one who had to capture the flies, which I didn't think was fair because the others could have used their powers to capture some. It was stupid and it really annoyed me. It was probably so I would stop being anxious and stayed out of their hair, but still.

"Why don't I remember?" Hera asked. "This makes little sense."

Hermes sighed. "Well… what happened was I came barging in through that broken door over there, and you were just about to leave when the door hit you in the head really hard and knocked you out. Some of your memory is probably fuzzy because of that."

There was silence for a moment, as if she was trying to deduce that was, in fact, true. Luckily the door was in fact broken, so the story appeared true.

"I guess that makes sense. Besides, Hermes, you wouldn't have reason to lie to me, now would you?"

"No, ma'am. I serve you and your husband with all my strength."

"He won't be my husband much longer. What will you do then?"

Hermes paused. "I will still serve the both of you,

of course."

"Excellent answer. Now, please help me up."

I could hear shuffling as he must have been helping her up. "Now, what should we do with these flies?"

"Up to you, my queen. Do as you wish."

"You mean to tell me you don't have a soft spot for any of them, not even the boy whom the daughter of Hades loves?"

"Why would I? He is just a human. I wouldn't have even considered him a threat and don't understand why you would have come down here to deal with them. It seems like a waste of time."

Hera laughed. "I knew it was, but after hearing what Aphrodite said about them, I started to worry. If I didn't come down, perhaps someone would have helped them. I can't let this wedding fall apart, Hermes, you know how long I have wanted a divorce from Zeus?"

"A long time?" Hermes asked.

"A very long time. I need a break from him, it's all about sex, either with me or some other woman. It doesn't matter whether they are human, goddess, or some weird creature. He wants to fuck them all."

I didn't need the reminder, especially since Chrys was already in Olympus. I prayed to god that he hadn't tried anything yet. Although, I had a feeling if he did, Chrys would have snapped and perhaps killed him. That definitely hadn't happened, so we were probably safe so far.

"He is known as being a hoe," Hermes commented. "But you two used to be in love. You used to get jealous if any other woman even looked at Zeus a certain way."

"That was a long time ago, back when my heart wasn't as wounded. After so many years of dealing with his shit, I decided maybe it was time to move on. It was time to just let him go."

It was a little sad to hear someone say that about the person they used to love. I knew that I would never lose my love for Chrys, even if we were together for eternity. If Hades could love Persephone after the way she treated him for so long, I could love someone like Chrys who I knew would always love me in return.

Hermes went on. "Well, let's get back. You are probably tired after such an intense spell."

"Yeah, we should go. But first, let out those flies so they may wander for an eternity. It isn't like anyone will miss any of them."

"As you wish."

Man, she was such a bitch. She would do that to

people she hardly knew? Hell, she might have known some of these other gods and just didn't care. That was rough to hear. I glanced at the others who looked pissed and a little scared. If we got caught, we might be royally screwed.

So, the goal was not to get caught, and to make sure she doesn't kill us when we succeeded in helping Chrys. Cool.

We all held on as the bag shifted and Hermes carried us. I had no idea how long it would take to get to Olympus, if it was an instantaneous thing, or if we had to travel for a long while. I didn't even know where Olympus was. Was it in the sky? Was it another dimension, was it sort of like the Underworld where it's there, but isn't? So many questions I didn't want to ask in fear Hera might overhear us.

Later. I would get those answers, eventually.

We were jostled around for a good hour. None of us puked, but I sure wanted to. I was glad I didn't have a full stomach, or I might have. Hermes would have been pissed, I bet, and would probably make me buy him a new bag. Where did he even get this bag, anyway? I bet it had some sentimental value and he would have said it was priceless. Then he would have had me pay even more.

No, I couldn't barter. I didn't have any money.

I wished I could talk to the others to help soothe my nerves, but we all had to stay quiet to make sure Hera didn't hear us. Safety first, comfort second, I supposed. I just hoped it wouldn't be much longer as I was sick of this already.

After a few more moments, it felt as if we had stopped. I glanced up through the small opening between the bag and the cover to find clear blue sky. It smelt of ocean now, which made no sense to me, but it was refreshing.

Well, we weren't in London anymore, that was for sure.

"It's good to be back home, isn't it, Hermes?" I heard Hera say.

"Yes, it is."

"It's so much more beautiful here than the mortal realm. The humans have wrecked the place, I don't even vacation there anymore. It's sickening."

"I agree, ma'am."

"But anything is better than the Underworld. You go the most often, other than Persephone. What do you think, is it as bad as everyone says?"

"It is very dreary. Only Hades would be mad enough to stay there."

She laughed. "Well, it isn't as if he has much of a

choice. No, he didn't have a choice when Zeus assigned him down there. It was a marvelous idea, too. It wasn't like any of us cared for that brother of ours. He was always judging our ways and causing trouble. Sticking him down there was the smartest idea Zeus ever had."

Damn, poor Hades. I knew he liked it down there, even if they forced him, as he didn't have to deal with this lot. But damn, they were all assholes. I felt I could relate, though, as none of my family or so-called friends ever wanted anything to do with me and just used me for their own devices.

I guess I had a lot in common with Hades. Maybe that was why he kept me around.

Also, the Underworld wasn't dreary. It was spectacular if you gave it a chance. Sure the castle Hades had looked like something out of a horror film, and it was always dark, but once your eyes adjusted and Chrys stopped playing vampire pranks on you, it wasn't that bad. Not everything had to be sex and drugs, although I couldn't talk since I got into Hades' stash... and slept with his daughter.

There was more walking and I could now tell we were definitely somewhere warmer and I could take my coat off without freezing. There was silence for a while when I heard Hera's voice once again.

"Oh Persephone, just the goddess I wanted to see."

We all froze. Was this a good thing or a bad thing? Did we want to run into her when we were still with Hera? I guess at least that meant we were close and didn't have to travel much further.

"Yes, my queen?" Persephone asked.

"I wanted to tell you that your little plan failed, and that human and those gods that were helping are gone. Good luck ever finding them again, they are lost forever."

"I don't know what you are talking about, ma'am. What human and gods?"

Hera laughed. "Nice try, but I know you were working with them to stop this wedding. Your plan failed and this wedding will go through."

There was a brief pause of silence and then Persephone replied. "When my daughter marries Zeus, you realize you will no longer be queen. We will see if anyone stays at your side and grovels at your feet. My guess is that they will all turn their backs on you, and you will be nothing but a sad, old hag."

I wanted to clap so badly. Damn, that was a good burn. I glanced at the others who were also smiling, impressed that she would say something so biting to Hera.

"How dare you, Persephone! Wait until Zeus hears what you said to me!"

"As if he'll care."

"Now, ladies," Hermes stopped them from going on. "This is no place for a fight. Persephone, you will see Chrys later, yes? Well, I got her some souvenirs so please take her this bag. And Hera, let's go to Zeus. We can tell him what happened and maybe he will in fact scold Persephone. Who knows with him?"

He handed the bag off into the hands of Persephone. We were that much closer to saving Chrys.

Chapter 19

CHRYS

Mother left me alone in her apartment to go find Hermes, just to be on the safe side. I was to stay here in case he came here first. We got word that Hera was back, and since I was worried, she figured it would be easiest to go to Hermes rather than for him to come straight here. He was crafty, we both knew, but that didn't mean he could get away from scrutiny for too long. I just had to promise that I wouldn't move from my spot, which was mother's apartment.

I stared out the window, wondering if everything ended up fine. I felt that Huntley was okay and that everything would be fine. He was close to me and they say sometimes one could feel if someone was okay or not if your love for them was strong enough. I felt my love was strong enough for Huntley and therefore knew he'd survive.

Pacing around in front of the balcony, I tried to take in the fact I would have to fake marry Prometheus. Was that even a good idea? Was that what I wanted? Marrying one god for another? Or at least, a titan. I didn't know Prometheus well—I didn't know many people well—and I worried he was just like the others. Father trusted him, and Huntley did too, so he couldn't be too bad. Mother seemed to trust him, but I didn't trust her taste in men. But according to the others, they thought he was good.

But why did I feel in my gut something more was going on?

It was probably because I didn't want to trust anyone else, not after what A.J. did to me. We had been friends for centuries, and he had been using me all that time. It seemed like every god I had met wanted to use me one way or another. That is all they ever did.

Which was why my father didn't fit in—which is why I didn't fit in. We didn't play games with people and believe they were all tools for our own selfish gain. We cared about people. I didn't realize how rare that was for gods until now.

I heard a knock on the door and froze. It wouldn't have been mother since she had a key. I didn't know if I should open it or not. The answer was probably not.

"Hey, Persephone, are you in there?" It was Apollo. Shit, I would not answer if it was him. I didn't want to deal with his shit.

I ignored the knock and stayed quiet. "I could just use my card if you don't open the door."

His card? Why would he have a card? Did my mother know that? Was I wrong to think my mother was better than him and he and her hooked up?

Either way, I had to figure out what I wanted to do as I didn't want him to open the door to find me standing there. No, I would open the door and make him go away.

Opening the door, I found Apollo there, his hands in his jean pockets and smiling. "Where's your mom?"

"She's gone. What do you want?" I asked, not willing to take any of his shit.

He leaned against the doorframe. "Why are you so hostile towards me? I have done nothing wrong."

"You tried to get me to join your wolf orgy."

Apollo rolled his eyes. "That's not what it was.

Besides, you were the one that was on something. You've got to tell me, what was it? Looked pretty strong."

I shook my head. "I don't know what you are talking about."

He laughed. "I've tried more things than you would ever know. Now come on, spill it. Did someone get into her daddy's stash?"

I shot him a look. "What do you want?"

"I just wanted to talk to your mother about something I overheard. Something about Hera."

How did he know about Hera? And what did he even care? It wasn't like he was on my side, nor even know about Huntley and the others, so how would he know…

Maybe he was watching us more than we knew.

"What about her?" I asked. Maybe I could get a little information about what he knew that way."

"I just heard a rumor she was going to the mortal realm to deal with some pests. Something about them wanting to stop this wedding. Know anything about it?" he asked.

I did not like what I was hearing. He knew too much, and I wondered if he knew more than he was letting on. But how? "I don't know what you are talking about."

"Well, then I guess there is nothing to discuss then."

I started to close the door when he put his foot in the way. "Hey, you are the one who said there wasn't anything else to discuss."

"I meant about Hera. I do, however, want to know more about you. It amazes me that Zeus can be so scared about a young goddess like yourself."

"What, are you going to get me to use my powers and get me killed? Is that it?"

He laughed. "No, I heard what you did to Poseidon and I prefer not to keep dying and getting brought back to life. No, I just want to know how your father did it—how was he able to hide you for so long. And your mom. Not a peep from her. She and I go way back, you know."

"Yeah, I know. She hit you in the head with a magazine. Tells me what kind of character you are really like."

"She's just playful. You know, I knew her before her and your father ever met. At one time, I thought the two of us could be a couple."

Now he was just pissing me off more than he already was. What the hell was he even trying to get at? Why did he think I wanted to hear about how he wanted to be with my mom before she married my father? "Can you just take your foot out of the door jam? I'm kind of done talking to you."

"I will move my foot if you let me in."

I laughed. "I'm not letting you in."

"Oh, come now, you might like to hear what I have to say."

I pushed on the door, squeezing his foot in the frame. "Not interested."

"Even if it has to do with that human you care so much about?"

This time, I flung open the door, shoved him as hard as I could, and then slammed the door shut. I had a feeling the only reason he came over was to see what information he could get from me, and then would tell Zeus. No, I wouldn't let him find out anything about Huntley or the others.

And I had a feeling he was lying about the key card too. He knew Persephone and was trying to get me to talk.

There was a knock at the door. I ignored it. Another knock. Would he ever let up?

"Honey, I need to talk to you," I could hear the voice from the other side of the door. It wasn't Apollo, but Demeter.

I guess I could open it and tell her that mother had gone out for a while. I opened the door. The moment she saw me, she gave me a look of disgust. Such a grand family reunion.

"Where is Persephone?" She asked, not even a hello or anything. I debated if I enjoyed talking to her or Apollo more. Right now, the dial was pointing more at Apollo.

"She is out, she will be back later, but I can tell her you came by."

"How long will she be?"

Was she not going to end with the questions? I shrugged. "I don't know, not too long so she can come find you after she gets back."

She forced me forward into the room and walked in. "I'll wait."

I let out a sigh. Hopefully mother wouldn't bring the others with her, otherwise Demeter might tell on us. Between her and Apollo, why was there always something to stress out about?

"Can I get you anything?" I asked in a fake cheery voice. At least I could try to act kind, mainly so mother wouldn't scold me.

"Water would be lovely." She still didn't look me in the eye as she sat down.

I got some water for both of us. At least this would kill time, but I felt like it would just make time go even slower. I handed her the water, and she took it without a thank you. She really was pretentious. I could see where my mother sometimes got that from, and I could see how these people would make her feel like she was going insane—I knew any longer with them and I would snap.

Sitting down on a different couch, because I had a feeling she didn't want me near her, we sat in silence, sipping on our waters. I debated saying anything, wondering if I should just make conversation or if I should keep silent. I wasn't one to keep silent, as it made me feel awkward.

"I don't understand why Persephone holds you so dear like she does." She broke the silence. I didn't know what to say to that, as it was a total bitch comment. So, I didn't respond, because everything I would have to say would just end in an all-out yelling match. I didn't feel like dealing with that today.

She went on. "Having to carry a daughter of Hades all by her lonesome must have been difficult. That bastard made her carry you without telling anyone, not even her own mother. My dear daughter was probably miserable the entire time and he just made it worse."

I clenched my free hand into a fist. I had to

remember, I couldn't punch my grandmother in the face. I couldn't.

Man, when did I start becoming like Huntley? Maybe my mother was right, maybe the two of us were a lot alike.

"Then he hid you from all of us, and trained you to be a dark, brooding mess, just like him. He knew you shouldn't have existed, that you were a curse for us gods, yet he didn't even care and raised you, anyway. He should be punished for what he did, but instead Zeus just thinks with his dick and decides to marry you."

She wasn't wrong on that last part, but she didn't know my father—none of them did. They all assumed he was some horrible monster when he was the kindest god out there.

I slammed my glass of water on the table. "How dare you speak of him that way!"

Demeter gasped, as if she didn't expect me to speak. "Excuse me?"

"He has done everything he can for my mother and for me. He knows you all just think for yourselves and tried to protect me from all your shit! I was happy when I was in the Underworld—I had everything I could have ever dreamed of! So did mother, but the fact she had to come back to you lot made her miserable beyond belief! You all have never taken the time to listen to my mother or my father! You just assumed she was miserable and made more mess for them and caused them to grow apart!"

She stood up and pointed at me. "How dare you speak to me that way! I am the Goddess of Harvest and Agriculture, one of the oldest gods in Olympus! Can you imagine what it would be like to be the Goddess of Harvest and have your daughter taken away by the God of Death? He is the complete opposite of what my daughter should have been with! Hell, my daughter shouldn't have married any god, none are good enough for her! But no, he kidnapped her and forced her to commit with him! Giving her the pomegranate of the Underworld! You know what that does to someone?"

I didn't answer, but just glared at her. Half because I didn't want to, and the other half not wanting her to know that I had experienced the pomegranates from the Underworld.

Demeter went on. "It makes them not think straight, and they get infatuated with everything around them! He tricked her!"

I didn't know how to respond. I knew about the pomegranates causing a psychedelic effect, although

I didn't know that played a part in their marriage. I couldn't see my father giving mother those seeds to trick her though, as I didn't even know about the seeds until Huntley found them. Mother admitted to me she had fallen for him all those years ago, so why did they think he had used those to trick her? To drug her?

I stood up, slamming my hands on the table. "My father would never do that! If mother had any of those seeds, it was by her own choice! He didn't force her to do anything!"

Demeter was screaming hysterically now. "He kidnapped my daughter and I will never forgive him for that! I mourn each and every year for her! It is not fair she is stuck with that monster!"

The door opened and we both found Persephone standing there. She looked shocked. I wondered how much she heard from outside the door.

"Mother, what are you doing here?" She asked Demeter.

"I came looking for you, seeing if you wanted to go shopping but this atrocity was here instead. I don't know how you can stand having a daughter so much like your husband around. She is as disrespectful as him."

Persephone took a deep breath. "Mother, I need to

you to leave right now."

"Why, I waited for you. Don't you want to come with me?"

"Right now, I don't want to speak to you. Don't you ever call my daughter an atrocity. Leave before I snap."

Demeter looked horrified and stormed away. I sat down and rubbed my face with my hands. I wanted to hurt her. It took everything to keep my power from taking over. I could feel it at the end of my fingertips, though, wanting to destroy.

Maybe I was the monster everyone made me out to be.

I took a breath, shaking off the feeling. "Damn, mother, how can you put up with her? She is so negative all the time."

Persephone closed the door. "You get used to it. Forget about her. Hermes gave me this bag. I presume it's enchanted."

She sat next to me and opened it. I gasped, not believing what I saw.

"Huntley?!"

Chapter 20

HUNTLEY

I looked up to find Chrys' smiling face. Giant smiling face. At the moment, I didn't care what size she was; I was just happy to see her face. It had been so long; we had come so far. We were finally in the home stretch to save her.

Maybe this plan would work

One problem I saw in the near future was trying to figure out how to get back to normal size. Did either of them know how to fix this or was this just Hermes' magic? If that was the case, then how long would it take for him to come back and help us?

"Huntley!" Chrys yelled when she saw us. "Oh my god, how are you that small? How did you even get in here? And…" Chrys frowned. "Why the fuck is A.J. with you?"

That would take some time to explain. I shrugged. "Long story. Do you guys know how to make us normal?"

Persephone peeked inside the bag. "Yeah, just give us a minute. First, we need to get you out of there. I don't think Hermes would appreciate us ruining his bag."

Chrys carefully picked me up. It was odd, to have the girl you loved hold you in her hands like some kind of hamster. She placed me on the ground and then she grabbed A.J. and flung him at the wall as hard as she could. He screamed as he went through the air like some doll and hit the wall with a soft thud. A.J. bounced down to the ground, rolling to where I was standing, groaning.

He deserved it.

"Mother, can we keep A.J. small? I would like to keep him in a cage and torture him if that's all right? Maybe with the sun and a magnifying glass."

That was my Chrys. I smiled, happy to hear her think of ways to torture A.J.. She seemed to have her spunk back.

Persephone shook her head. "No, when I undo the spell it will turn them all back to regular size."

Damn, I really wanted to keep A.J. in a small glass

cage that I could shake around. Once we were all out, Persephone snapped her fingers. We all returned to our regular sizes. A.J. still lay on the floor, bent over in pain.

Chrys ran straight to me and wrapped her arms around me. I held her tight and kissed her straight on the lips. She kept her hands around me and I twirled her hair with my finger.

"I missed you so much, Huntley. I'm so glad you made it out safe. I was so worried."

I squeezed her tighter. "It's all right, we are all here. I promised you I would keep you safe, didn't I?"

She laughed and I could see tears forming in her eyes. "Yeah, you did."

We held each other a little longer, ignoring the fact that everyone was staring at us. I didn't care. They should understand. Everything we were doing was for her.

And now we were this much closer to saving her.

Chrys backed up a little and smiled. "You haven't changed a bit. How was staying in the mortal realm?"

I shrugged. "It was okay, nothing compared to the Underworld. I had some shitty roommates."

Mel shot daggers with her eyes while Pothos

came over and smacked me on the back of the head.

"Ow," I said. "It was a joke! I swear!"

"You better be, or I swear if you have to stay any longer in my apartment, I will be a roommate from hell."

"And I am an amazing roommate. I could easily make your life a living hell if I wanted," Mel added.

Would I have to stay with them longer? With everything going on, I forgot that Chrys would marry Prometheus and I had no idea where they would go from there. Maybe I would still have to room with him until things settled.

Ugh.

I turned to Chrys and realized she didn't know that part of the plan. "Hey, Chrys, listen… We have a way to get you out of this marriage, but—"

"But I have to marry Prometheus." She glanced over at Prometheus. "My mother has told me what the plan was." She turned back to me for a sec. "And I agree to it."

I didn't know if I felt relieved or not. I was glad that we were saving her, but at what cost? Prometheus didn't seem like he actually wanted to marry her, as in be with her like that, but what if he tried something? What if he wasn't as innocent as we all believed he was?

What if he had an alternative motive?

I couldn't believe I was having second thoughts now that we were at the moment I had been hoping for. In reality, I wanted to whisk her away right then and there and not deal with any god ever again. But that wouldn't happen, because the reality was I wasn't strong enough to keep her safe and Prometheus was.

I glanced over at Mel. What did she think about all of this? I mean, she and Prometheus were a couple, kind of, or did she understand it was just a fling and Prometheus didn't care about her? Or would she not care if he was married, as most gods didn't seem to. So far, I hadn't heard a peep out of her about it.

Prometheus clapped his hands together. "Great, then we should get everything set. When will Hades be joining us? We need him as a witness, since he is the God of the Underworld, after all."

Persephone answered. "He should be here tomorrow for some wedding planning he needs to be present for. We should be able to do it then."

Prometheus nodded. "We will have to hide in the meantime. Persephone, do you think it would be a problem if we stayed here?"

She hesitated. "The problem is Demeter, she

sometimes comes by here and she might see you, although I did just piss her off and I doubt she will come back for a while."

"We could split up," Chrys said. "Huntley stays with me and everyone else can stay here."

I liked the plan and looked at the others for support. Then it would just be her and I in her room. All night. Oh, for the love of god, someone else please agree.

Persephone smiled a little, then shrugged. "I'm not sure how we would get you over there without being spotted. It isn't far but there are… some who have been keeping a close eye that I worry will either tell or blackmail us."

"Who?" Prometheus asked.

"Apollo. I think he knows something is up," Persephone sighed. I didn't like the sound of that.

Chrys bit her lip. "Actually, he was just here. He said he was looking for you, but I think he was trying to get information about what we were doing. He knew about Huntley and that Hermes was up to something."

Persephone pinched the bridge of her nose. "Of course. He's such a pain in the ass."

Great, more problems. Would they ever end?

"I don't think we have anything to worry about

with Apollo," Prometheus commented. "He and I go way back and he wouldn't stab me in the back. If he gives any more problems, let me talk to him."

Was that a good thing or a bad thing? If we had another in, then why didn't Prometheus reach out to Apollo earlier? Something wasn't adding up, but I decided not to bring it up. There was still too much in the air right now.

"That just leaves Demeter then," Pothos added. "I have a feeling she is still a nosy mom that gets all in your business, Persephone?"

Persephone rolled her eyes. "Don't even get me started. However, it seems that Chrys and her just got into a big argument and I added fuel to that fire. I think she will leave us alone for a couple of days, which should give us enough time."

"Well then, do you suggest we all stay here?" Prometheus asked.

Persephone nodded. "I think that is the best idea, until Hades comes, especially since he will come straight to this apartment, anyway."

"Will you mind if all five of us stay in here though?" Prometheus asked. "Do you have enough pillows?"

"We will figure it out. But we might figure out a way to get Huntley to Chrys' room. It just might not be until early morning when no one is out. Or when Hermes comes back, he might be able to do something. He will probably be awhile, though, as Hera is complaining about me to Zeus. She might get distracted, though, she usually does. Then Zeus will make a comment and there will be an argument. Hopefully there is no big fight today," Persephone explained with a little sigh.

"What exactly happened?" Chrys asked. "How were you all able to get away from Hera?"

"Well," I began. "It all started with running into A.J. while I was around London."

"Buying comics," Pothos added.

I gave him a look. "Getting my mind off everything and you suggested I go buy comics, yes. Then I saw A.J. outside the store. I tried to beat him into a pulp, but can't because he's immortal. Then I brought him to our place—"

"My place." Pothos interrupted. I gave him another look.

"Anyway, we found out he was working for Poseidon who is working on a plan for when you are on your way back to the Underworld, which we'll need to figure out later. Then Prometheus got mad A.J. wasn't answering our questions, he seemed to be lying to us when he did. So

Prometheus stabbed him in the eyes with an ice pick."

Chrys turned to Prometheus. "I like you already."

"Then as we sat down, Hera came and said she didn't want this wedding stopped and was about to curse us all when Prometheus stopped her by making her drink a drop of Lethe. Then Hermes came in, all song and dance, which was strange. Then he shrunk us and put us in the bag and told Hera that she had turned us into flies."

Persephone and Chrys looked very confused with all the information that we gave them.

Chrys was the first to answer. "So... A.J. came back, but to betray me again?"

I nodded. "Yup, seems so."

She turned to where A.J. was still laying on the ground. "I wonder what his plan was."

"We were going to figure that out when he could talk again. Stabbing him in the eyes made it hard for him to talk." Prometheus explained. "But we do know it had something to do with Poseidon."

"That makes sense. He's his daddy's little helper, after all." Chrys said as she walked over to A.J.. She kicked him in the stomach as hard as she could. I was pretty sure I heard ribs crack. "Hey dick, wake up."

A.J. moaned as he stirred. "Just kill me now."

"I can't," Chrys said. "You were granted immortality by Zeus himself for betraying me. Otherwise you would be dead."

"Well, that isn't exactly true, you could kill me if you wanted. You have that power, which is the problem." He was able to cough out.

She kicked him in the stomach again. "I think I like the alternative of just hurting you for a long while."

"Understandable," A.J. moaned.

"We will have a long talk later, but first I am supposed to be meeting with the wedding coordinator for picking out some flowers or something. My mother is supposed to come along. We don't want to appear as if something is up," she said with a sad tone.

Persephone nodded. "Yeah, that is a good idea."

"Well, we will all be waiting," Prometheus said. "And we can finish up everything tonight."

Mel walked over to A.J.. "And I will give this guy some nightmares he will never forget. Then by the time you are back, he will pour his guts out."

Chrys nodded as she headed out the door. "Oh, also, don't open the door for anyone, even if you are friends with that wolf guy."

Wait, what?

Chapter 21

CHRYS

I tried to hide my excitement. The man I loved was finally in my reach. I was so happy that Hera didn't destroy him, or curse him, or whatever she would do with him. They could defeat her without Hermes' help. I was so glad.

The excitement often turned to worry, especially for Huntley. What if someone found out about him? Did Zeus know everything that went on in Olympus? Were humans even allowed to be here? I guessed it didn't matter if he was human or not, it just mattered that it was a human that wanted to stop the wedding.

Father would be here tomorrow, and everything would be fine. It couldn't be hard to hide them for a day, could it? I thought back to the fact that Apollo and Demeter barged into my mother's room like they owned the place. What if they did it again?

I didn't like the fact Prometheus seemed like he was friends with Apollo. Something about that seemed off. Apollo kept joking with me, teasing me, and pressing me for more information. Something about him didn't seem right, as if he was trying to come up with some kind of plan. Was Prometheus trustworthy if he worked with someone like that?

I tried to calm down and follow my mother's example. She seemed unphased, acting like her normal self. It was probably because she was used to being fake around all of these people. It was second nature for her.

Oh no, would I turn into my mother if I married Prometheus? Would I have to be fake around everyone?

I shook my head. No, I wouldn't, because I would do the opposite of her: I would fake my love for Prometheus instead of faking my hatred for him. But what if I started loving him? What would happen then?

And what about Huntley?

No, I needed to focus on the present. I couldn't worry about things that hadn't even happened yet. I had to worry more about the present and keeping them safe. They would be safe in mother's room, I just had to focus on that.

I wish Huntley could have stayed in my room with me, though. I would have felt safer with him close, and I wouldn't have to worry about anyone coming in as much. I mean, it meant Apollo was next door, and Huntley would have to suffer through hearing the weird noises with me, but I would feel safer knowing Huntley was with me. And we could take some pomegranates and let the night pass us by.

Mother and I went to where the caterer was located. It was near where we picked out the cake, or at least I thought it was. I got turned around in this place, even after the few days I had been venturing around in it.

From what I knew, Zeus wasn't supposed to come, and would be too busy with Hera to have time to come help with the arrangements. It relieved me, and I felt like I could go on for the rest of eternity without having to ever see him again. Maybe I wouldn't have to see him again after we left here.

With my luck, though, this wouldn't be the end.

"We are here," Persephone said as she opened a

door to a shop. A blue-skinned sprite got up and came to the door.

"Oh, you must be the bride-to-be of Zeus, Chrys, the daughter of Hades. It is a pleasure to meet you. Oh, and hello again Persephone."

"Hello, Krissy."

"I am so glad you came here for all the catering."

My mother seemed to genuinely smile. "Well this is one of the best restaurants in Olympus. Besides, Zeus demanded it. He loves your cooking, you should be proud."

Krissy blushed, clasping her hands together. "Thank you very much, I'm happy to hear that. I just hope we will make your big day special."

No, I think nothing would make that day special, or at least special in an enjoyable manner. Luckily it wouldn't happen, but at least I would get to try some excellent food.

Krissy brought out a giant platter full of small servings of different Greek foods. I gasped as I saw them all, ready for me to try. My stomach grumbled at the sight of them. I guess I forgot to eat lunch, which was a good thing—now I could enjoy all of this without my stomach arguing with me.

First were the salads and spreads. First up was the horiatiki, which was the typical Greek salad with tomatoes, onions, cucumbers, olives, and feta cheese. I took a bite and found the feta to be the best cheese I had ever tasted. If the wedding would actually happen, I would want this on the list.

I wondered if Prometheus and I would have an actual wedding with food or if it would be something that we would hide with just a couple of us. From what I could figure out, it was just going to be in my mother's apartment. With Huntley standing there.

Was he really okay with all of this? The only reason I knew I could go along with it all was because of the fact he agreed to it. It would just be painful if I had to be away from Huntley any more than I already had been.

We tried a bunch more salads and spreads to the point where I thought my taste buds couldn't be more delighted, but they always were. I wished I could eat like this every day and realized that I did. I would just have to ask my father to make some of these meals. I was surprised he didn't serve more Greek food, but I guess he probably used to eat it all the time and got a little sick of it. Or maybe it just reminded him of Olympus.

Next we tried appetizers. My mouth was practically drooling with all the choices they gave me. I was so happy that Zeus wasn't here to ruin all of this for me. If he were here, I would have lost my appetite and everything would have tasted like my freedom being taken away. Although, I had to remember, all this food I was tasting wasn't going to be for anything.

Or, at least, I hoped.

I fell in love with the dolma, which were stuffed grape leaves. Grape plants were so crazy as they produced so much food substance. I loved grapes, and those were something my father included in his meals, but I never knew that the leaves could be used in cooking. I ate half a dozen of them before my mother elbowed me in the stomach.

"Sweetie, don't fill up, we still have to try the main courses."

I nodded. "Right. Sorry, they were just so good."

Mother smiled. "You surprise me, your father always hated Greek food. I thought maybe you would have the same tastes as him."

I shrugged and whispered, "He didn't like the people here, not the food itself."

She laughed, "yeah, I suppose that's true."

An enormous platter of fresh foods were brought out to us. Mother was right, I shouldn't have eaten so many of the appetizers but I just couldn't help myself. I stared at them, more drool dripping down my face.

The sprite smiled. "Enjoy. Let me know if you have questions about any of the entrees."

I nodded. "Thank you."

She let us be while we tasted them all. The first one I tried was the moussaka, which was a casserole with eggplant. It was tasty, as I didn't like most of the recipes with eggplants that my father had made. This was phenomenal.

I tried a bit of everything she brought out and then some desserts that would be served before the cake. If this wedding would have been a thing, then I would probably eat myself into a coma, and then just never wake up.

"Well, flower, what are your favorites?" Persephone asked. I bit my lip.

"I liked the moussaka, lokma, dolma, and gigandes for sure. The horiatiki salad would be good as well. Then we have the cake, so for anything else you can pick mother."

"Kolokithokeftedes and spanakorizo," mother added. "Those are always a favorite." I noticed my mom liking the zucchini fritters and spinach and rice dish, and they were delicious. I nodded, seconding the motion, not that it would matter, but I made a note of all the names to have the cooks in the Underworld to make for me. I didn't care if father hated it.

The sprite wrote down our choices. "All right, I will get those down. Thank you for coming in and trying everything."

"Thank you for making everything," I said. "Give my compliments to the chef."

She smiled. "I will. Have a splendid day."

With that, we left the shop and I rubbed my full stomach. I felt a bit bad that this wedding wouldn't happen, as all that food would be wasted, but the wedding would be canceled before any real preparations.

I couldn't wait to get back to Huntley, but wondered if anyone would notice my mother and I were hanging around each other more than normal. I hadn't been here long, and it wasn't like many would take notice. It wasn't odd that a daughter was hanging out with her mother, was it? I didn't want to seem suspicious, but anything I did felt out of the ordinary. All I could think about was Huntley and how we would get out of this.

As for A.J., I didn't know what I would do with him. If given the chance, he would probably bring all my hopes and dreams crashing down. Again. I hated him for what he had done, and the fact he thought he could screw me over again. I wanted to make him pay.

But I couldn't use my powers without a big red flag going up. That red flag almost went up when I was fighting Artemis, but I wanted to point out it was for self-defense. That girl was crazy. She liked her brother way too much.

"What should I do about A.J., mother?" I asked in a whisper so no one around could hear us. "I want him dead, but I can't exactly do that."

She shrugged. "Do whatever you want to do, sweetie. You are a grown adult, or goddess, you have the power to do what you want."

"Except for actually using my powers. If I did that, Zeus will destroy me."

"Yes, but you could curse him, or injure him again and again until the end of time. It's your choice."

"I can't do anything just yet, though, since no one knows he is here. But after everything blows over, I might drag him down to the Underworld myself. Or maybe just into the water and watch him drown for eternity."

Mother patted my head. "That's my daughter."

As we rounded a corner, we found Apollo leaning against the wall. When he saw us, he smiled.

"About time, I thought maybe you forgot all about your precious friends."

I froze. Shit, this guy was a pain. "What are you talking about?"

"Prometheus and the others. They are here, right?"

"What do you want, Apollo?" Mother growled.

"Don't worry, I won't tell Zeus. But I do want a word with Prometheus. He and I are old buddies and I'm curious what he has been up to these past days."

Mother took in a deep breath and I could tell she was debating what to do. It was clear Apollo knew they were here and if he didn't get what he wanted, he could turn us in.

"If you promise to keep your mouth shut, I'll see what I can do."

He grinned. "Thank you, Persephone, you are an enormous help."

Apollo was up to something and I didn't like it. I hoped Prometheus could talk to him and figure it out before it was too late. However, the fact he seemed chummy with Prometheus made me question Prometheus a bit more.

Mother shoved past him, and we went back to her apartment without saying a word.

Chapter 22

HUNTLEY

I peeked out the door to see if Chrys and Persephone were back yet. I didn't see anyone except a few other gods walking around. There were some other beings too, but I had no idea what they were called. They all seemed to go about their day as I found myself stuck in Persephone's apartment with the others.

It took a bit, but it hit me—I was in Olympus.

This was the heaven of the Greek religion. It was crazy to even think about. I mean, I guess I spent time in the Underworld with Hades, but this was like… only where gods were supposed to go. In fact, I might have been the only human to have ever been to Olympus. I wondered what other gods would think of me if they knew I was here?

Probably kill me in an instant.

It surprised me that I could get in undetected. Would there not be a human detector of sorts? Could humans have come here if given the chance earlier? Kind of like Persephone sneaking in a human to the Underworld? Did that mean other gods snuck humans up here?

I wished Chrys would come back so these questions would stop filling my head.

Peeking around the outside again, I wondered if Ares and Aphrodite came back up here. Zeus invited everyone to the wedding, so perhaps they were.

Prometheus hit me in the head with a magazine.

I turned around and glared at him. "What was that for?"

"Stop sticking your head in the window or someone will see us. You don't look like Persephone and although she sneaks men into the Underworld, I doubt she does up here."

I backed away from the window. He had a point, but I was impatient. I was here and could see Chrys only to have to wait again. I hated this, why couldn't anything ever just go as planned.

I guess it wasn't against our actual plan, but my

plan was once I saw Chrys again, I would never leave her side. Yet, within an hour of seeing her, I was separated from her yet again. This blew hard.

Honestly, I hoped that I would get to stay in her room. It wasn't like I wanted to do anything, but I just wanted to hold her close all night—to know she was safe. But now it sounded like I wouldn't be able to, at least not tonight. I guess one more night of waiting wouldn't hurt. I was close enough to know she was safe.

"Why don't you think Persephone sneaks men in her room up here?" I asked. I didn't care, but I figured the conversation could pass the time.

"Because, she could have any god up here if she wanted. And because there is a harsher punishment for sneaking in humans compared to the Underworld. Hades is a softy when it comes to her and Chrys. No one else, though."

That made sense, I supposed. Hades was soft with Persephone and Chrys. I had seen him let Persephone get away with a lot, just because he loved her. Well, more because he didn't want to deal with her anymore. I doubted his love had ever changed though, even after all that she had done.

I took a seat on the couch and tried to take a deep breath. I just wanted all of this to be over.

A.J. stirred again, and I got up and kicked him in the stomach again. One of us would get up when he woke and hurt him until he passed out. It was mainly because we didn't want him to yell for someone outside, and because we couldn't find any duct tape. That, or we were just having too much fun hurting him. Probably just the latter. Pothos got up and helped me this time, giving him a good hit to the head and he slumped over again.

Taking my seat back on the couch, I bounced my legs, letting the energy I had pent up dissipate that way. It wouldn't work, but I did it anyway as I wondered how much longer Chrys and Persephone would be. I hoped it wasn't much longer, as I felt as if I couldn't wait another minute. I tried to pass the time checking out Persephone's place, which was like something out of an older city in Greece. It made sense, since they were gods of Greece. It was just after being in the Underworld, which wasn't anything like Greece but more like Transylvania, I was a little surprised by the contrast. Then again, I guess Hades was the odd duck in the family. Had to hand it to him, he stood his ground with all these gods for what he believed. None of them seemed as cool as him.

The door opened as Persephone and Chrys

walked in. I jumped up and embraced her, glad that she was back. I noticed she seemed a little uneasy.

"What is it?" I asked.

She hesitated for a moment. "Um… Apollo knows you all are here."

"What?" I asked. "Who's Apollo? Can we trust him?"

Everyone kind of shifted, as if they weren't sure how to answer that. I pinched the bridge of my nose. "Ah, so is that a no?"

Persephone shrugged. "Well, not necessarily. Prometheus, he wanted to talk to you alone. I'm not sure about what, but I presume about everything going on."

Prometheus nodded. "Okay. He and I go way back, I doubt we have to worry about him telling Zeus. He's pissed at Zeus because, well, he got screwed over, like most gods have. He most likely wants to help."

Chrys kind of scrunched her nose, as if she didn't believe that, but she said nothing.

Persephone let out a sigh. "I'm not sure how you are supposed to meet up with him, as I'm afraid someone will see."

"Don't worry, Persephone, I know how to make my way through Olympus without raising suspicion, and he knows I know where to meet up. I will go see him later tonight."

She nodded. I did not understand what was going on now, other than we had another god involved with our scheme. How many did that make now? I couldn't keep track. The more that knew, the more likely someone would tell Zeus what was going on. We just needed one more day, that way Hades would be here and help us finish everything. I believed it would be fine.

Who was I kidding?

"We should just focus on getting information out of A.J. for now," Chrys said with a slight smirk. "One problem at a time."

That seemed fair, and A.J. was stirring awake again. She bent down to where he was lying on the floor. "Oh, A.J., I have so many questions for you. Today will be a lengthy day for you."

He looked up at her "I'll tell you anything, Chrys, I've been through enough."

She smiled as she stroked his hair. "I disagree." With that, she grabbed his hair and pulled out a chunk. He screamed and with a snap of her fingers, duct tape appeared over his mouth. I wondered why none of the other gods did that earlier.

"No screaming," she said. "Just answers."

He whimpered and mumbled something under the tape. She ripped it off.

"What was that?" She asked.

"I said I can't give answers if you tape my mouth."

Chrys nodded. "Yeah, I suppose that is true." She snapped her fingers again. "But you also can't scream as loud as I take my revenge."

Tears fell down A.J.'s eyes as Chrys stood up. "I need some help getting him in a chair."

Prometheus and Pothos pulled him up and put him in a chair. Chrys snapped her fingers again, and he was tied quite tightly in the chair.

Damn, she was scary when she was angry. Although, in this case, she seemed calm as opposed to her fully unleashed wrath. I wasn't sure which was scarier: her wrath or just her fiery anger.

Grabbing a knife from the kitchen counter, she pointed it at A.J.. "Now, I will make a few incisions. I want you to know, I will not stop even if you beg. But you should know, once I am done, I will ask you some questions and if I'm not completely satisfied with the answer, then I will do all the same incisions again, but an inch deeper. Are we clear?"

He nodded.

Then she started cutting him slowly. I had to look

away as it was making me nauseous. Everyone else watched as if this was normal for them. It was both gross and unnerving. I knew he would heal, but it was still sickening. Part of me felt bad, even though most of me felt he deserved this. I hated him so much for what he had done to her and how all this was his fault, but I was still human—I still felt empathy. Apparently.

I guess gods didn't understand that feeling.

Chrys cut him up for a good hour before stopping. After he finished whimpering, she pulled off the tape.

"Now, tell me, what is this stuff I hear about telling Poseidon how I would escape here?"

He took a deep breath, wincing. "He wanted to know which path down from Olympus you would take, so he could ambush you. That, or what day you would leave so he could come here and put an end to it all. He doesn't want you marrying Zeus, so he would never tell him the plan, but he would attack halfway so he could try to kill you himself."

Chrys laughed. "He thinks he can take me on? Didn't he learn the first time?"

A.J. shrugged. "He isn't the brightest god, but my job was to just get the info."

"And betray me again?" Chrys asked with a little

half-smile, as if she thought him betraying her again was amusing.

"And not be anchored to the ocean floor for a few centuries, yes."

Chrys shrugged. "I mean, I could do that too. Poseidon isn't the only one to fear. All of us gods can fuck you up."

"So I've noticed."

Chrys kicked his leg. "Hey, don't get pissed at me, you are the one who could have spent eternity in paradise, yet you decided coming back to earth was a better plan. Seems to me you are wrong."

"You think the afterlife is enjoyable? You can't do anything there for all of eternity, just be in the same area forever. You think that is paradise?"

No one said anything. He had a point, but would that be better than the suffering he was going through right now? I would like to think it would. I could spend all my time in Hades' castle if it meant being with Chrys. A few years had already gone by before we made our way to London and it felt like it had only been two weeks. But as many of them pointed out, a human like me couldn't imagine eternity until a few centuries passed.

I couldn't wait to prove them wrong though. A human like me proving some gods wrong. It would be epic.

"So what have you told him?" Chrys asked. A.J. said nothing. Chrys sighed as she snapped her fingers and a piece of duct tape appeared on his mouth again.

She started stabbing deeper this time as his cries were muffled from underneath the tape. I looked away and prayed that I wouldn't barf this time. It would be so embarrassing since these gods seemed to feel there was nothing wrong with this. It scared me a little, especially since we were planning to piss off one of the most powerful gods in all existence.

But there was nothing to worry about, right? It was something I had to keep convincing myself as I watched each god take their turn torturing A.J..

Chapter 23

CHRYS

I sat in my room, thinking about all the things that had happened. I got harassed by Apollo and then my grandmother, Huntley came with other people to help stop the wedding from happening, had satisfying food, got harassed again by Apollo, and then I tortured A.J.. It was a long day and full of quite a few different things. I had swung from one mood to the next and felt as if I couldn't feel anything new today. It was strange.

And we didn't get to sneak Huntley into my room. I was pretty bummed about that scenario.

I didn't know how I felt about torturing A.J. like I did. I had done worse to others, using my powers to kill and reanimate, but this felt different. Using that knife made it feel a lot more personal and I was having mixed feelings about it. Adrenaline was still rushing through my bloodstream. I didn't know if I loved or hated the feeling. So much had happened that day, and I just didn't know how to process it all.

I also didn't know how to process Prometheus turning into a wolf and running off with Apollo somewhere. I had so many questions and yet none that I was brave enough to ask. I felt that Prometheus could handle Apollo and that he was no longer an actual threat. It would be fine. Hopefully.

A.J., on the other hand, was still a threat. Something seemed odd about him. Yes, he had lied to me for centuries and that I didn't know what he was thinking, but this time it was like… he was a completely different person. He was giving us information, but still holding on to something of actual value. I had stabbed him many times and he would act like he was spilling his guts, but then I would ask another question and there was almost a smirk about him.

There was something else going on and I wasn't sure what it was. But I could feel it.

Daylight came wafting in and I wondered if I even slept. I moaned as I stretched and got up. Today was the day we all had been waiting for and my heart felt as if it couldn't beat any faster.

Father would travel up here to, initially, help get things ready for the wedding with Zeus. Instead, in secret, we would be setting up a wedding with Prometheus and I was to wed him. Then we would take the evidence to Zeus, and he would have to call the entire thing off.

Or at least we hoped.

I changed into my clothes, a little black dress that almost looked like a sundress, headed towards my mother's apartment where everyone was already waiting. Then in a couple of hours, father would come and meet up with her there. As long as everything went according to plan.

My heart felt like it would jump out of my chest as I walked over to the apartment. I didn't see any sign of Apollo or Prometheus, which I wasn't sure was a good thing or not. Prometheus had probably already returned to my mother's apartment and perhaps settling down to go over the plan once more. Maybe. It was none of my business what happened between him and Apollo last night, as long as they didn't reveal the plan to Zeus.

I knocked on the door, and mother opened it. I rushed in to find everyone was there, even Prometheus. Huntley ran over, and we hugged. I didn't want to leave his arms, and just prayed that we could still be together after all of this was through.

"How did the talk go? What is Apollo going to do?" I asked.

Prometheus shook his head. "Nothing, he is with us. He doesn't want to see Zeus get his way and wanted to make sure we would screw him over. If we need any help, he said to just ask."

For some reason, that felt right, even if unconvincing. I glanced over at A.J., who was still tied to the chair with tape over his mouth. Most of his wounds had already healed.

Now we just had to wait for father.

A knock sounded on the door. I ran over and opened it to find my father standing in the doorway. I wrapped my arms around him.

"Father."

He kissed the top of my head and squeezed me tight. "My precious flower, how has everything been? Is everyone treating you fine?"

I shrugged. "As fine as they can. I don't like any of them."

"That's my girl." He turned to mother, and it was awkward as they didn't know how to greet each other. It had been months since they had seen each other, yet neither of them seemed to want to embrace. They were still fighting because of me.

Prometheus coughed. "So, how do you want to go about this?"

Hades turned to him. "You have the box I gave Huntley, yes?"

He nodded. "Yes, right here."

Prometheus held it up and smiled. "Should we take them now?"

Hades nodded. "Yes, that would be the best thing to do. Zeus will see you took them and partook in the ceremony. But you will have to spend that many months in the Underworld."

"Understood," Prometheus said as he opened the container. It was the pomegranate seeds.

Huntley and I both looked at each other, confused.

"Uh, father."

"Yes, my Flower?"

"Those are the pomegranate seeds you keep in your desk."

He hesitated. "Yes, they are used in ceremony for weddings, at least in my domain, which is rare. Your mother and I took three in our wedding after Demeter demanded she spent more time on Earth or

Olympus than the Underworld."

Huntley and I looked at each other again, both appearing a little panicked.

I hesitated, wondering if I should say it. I mouthed to Huntley, "What should we do?"

He shrugged and mouthed back, "I don't know."

We stared at each other for a moment.

I bit my lip. "So… if I, let's say, took some with someone in the Underworld…"

"You would be married," Hades answered. A second later he pinched the bridge of his nose. "No. No no no no no."

"What is it?" Prometheus asked.

Persephone started laughing. "And you two sealed the deal, didn't you?"

I blushed as Huntley and I nodded.

Mother had to hold back her giggling. "How many did you both take?"

Huntley and I pondered this thought, and I shook my head. "I have no idea."

Father looked like he was about to pull his hair out. "No. No no no no."

Huntley put his arm on Hades' shoulder. "I can call you papa now!"

I placed my hand over my mouth, not believing he just did that. Mother was laughing hard now, holding her stomach.

Father glared at him as Huntley backed away. "Don't you ever call me that again you stupid, stupid human."

"We didn't know," I said. "How does this even change anything?"

Prometheus rubbed his face. "Because now that means we can't convince Zeus that the two of us are married."

"But that means I'm already married and Zeus won't be able to go against that," I said.

Prometheus shook his head. "No, he wouldn't care if he was human, and he would more likely just kill both of you since Huntley can't do anything to stop your powers."

Great. We were back to square one.

Mother, after taking some deep breaths, was the first to come up with a plan. "They weren't actually going to get married, why can't they just take the seeds and try to convince Zeus otherwise?"

She had a point. I looked at the others for confirmation.

Prometheus shrugged. "I guess it is all we've got. What do you say, Hades?"

Father looked like he was still in shock with everything that had just happened. "Yeah, that could work. Just need to be convincing I suppose."

I could do this. I could pretend to be married to Prometheus. He seems like an agreeable guy, right? Everyone here trusted him, so he was fine.

"How many seeds?" Prometheus asked.

Hades shrugged. "As many as you want, I suppose. I would say three would convince Zeus."

We both took three seeds. I had never had more than one at a time and wasn't sure how it would affect me. I also felt strange taking these with so many people around. Usually it was just Huntley and I with some music. Last time was when I was alone in my room, and Apollo killed my mood. Was this going to be the same as that?

I swallowed the three seeds. Only one way to find out.

The feeling was instantaneous, but I tried not to act as chilled out as I typically did. It was as strange as I thought it would be with everyone in here. It felt like I was in my body, but not quite at the same time. I had to admit, it was different since this was more ceremonial than just relaxing after a long day. I didn't feel as confused as normal, as if the seeds were affecting me a bit differently.

This was really weird.

"Since Chrys is apparently already married, none

of this means a thing. But he can tell if you have taken them. Prometheus, you will have to stay in the Underworld three months of the year to convince him for quite a while. It is a lot better than most think it is. And you will be able to leave, unlike most," father said.

Prometheus nodded. "Understood."

A.J. let out a muffled laugh. I forgot he was there since he had been in the background, making no noise.

Wait, all those years ago, when we first found the seeds, did he know and not say anything? He had gotten so mad at us about them, but he never told us why.

I ripped the tape off of his mouth. "Why didn't you say anything?"

He laughed. "Because Huntley was so desperate for a high, it was hilarious. He was just some stupid human that ended up marrying the daughter of Hades. Besides, I never thought he would consummate it. If you two just didn't have sex, it wouldn't have counted. I should have figured a daughter of Persephone wouldn't be able to keep her pants on for that long. I mean, even we almost —"

I punched him straight in the jaw. I couldn't

believe he was about to say what he was about to say. I didn't want father to know about it, and I was more pissed he said nothing to us. So many emotions were running through my mind.

Hades calmly walked over and stood in front of A.J.. Taking a deep breath, he grabbed A.J. by the throat and slammed him into the wall, chair and all. The chair, obviously, broke, and we would have to tie him to a new one. Splinters went flying across the room from the force father hit him against the wall with.

"What the hell are you doing here, A.J.?" Father growled.

With everything going on, he must have not noticed A.J. was in the room either. Funny how that happens.

"I'm under house arrest," he choked. "Been tortured for the past few days. It's great."

"He was trying to get information for Poseidon. He wants to ambush Chrys when she is leaving Olympus and try to kill her," Prometheus responded.

I glanced over to him to find his eyes a little red, almost as if he was out of it. First time was always the strongest, I had to agree. Enjoyable if it weren't for this company, though.

"When all of this is over, A.J., I'm dragging you down to Tartarus. You don't get to cross the Lord of the Underworld without consequences, do I make myself clear?"

"Please don't, I'll do anything."

"It's too late. Your judgement has already passed. Not even Zeus or your father can save you now. You should have just kept to yourself on Earth instead of going after my daughter again."

With a snap of his fingers, A.J. was bound up again to a new chair with tape over his mouth. Father dropped him to the ground and punched him in the stomach. It seemed like that was the thing to do.

Father turned to us. "Now, let us go to Zeus and get this over with."

Chapter 24

HUNTLEY

Prometheus, Hades, Chrys, and Persephone all left to go talk to Zeus. Pothos, Mel, and I were to stay and monitor A.J.. It made sense we had to stay back, as we weren't supposed to be in Olympus, anyway. We mostly came to just make sure everything ran smoothly, and more numbers if something did go wrong.

So to summarize: more waiting to endure.

At least this time Pothos pulled out a pack of Uno cards. I wasn't sure where they had been this entire time, because we had many chances to play Uno to pass the time, but I wouldn't complain. I knew if I said anything, he would hide them again so I would suffer more.

The three of us sat around a table and played a few games. We thought about including A.J., but decided we would all be pissed if he won. There was the other fact that none of us wanted to undo the ropes Hades had tied him up with so he could lift his arms, as they were super tight. We would need a saw to get them off.

At this point in the game, Mel had the least number of cards. I didn't care who won, as we were just trying to pass the time, but somewhere deep in my core, I wanted to win. I hadn't won against any of them for any game the entire time I had been in London and it was getting on my nerves. I didn't mind losing to Chrys, but there was no way I could lose this many times to these gods. It just wasn't fair. They had to be cheating and using their mind power to their advantage.

"No, we aren't using our mind powers Huntley, we are just that good," Pothos said. I glared at him.

I narrowed my eyes at him. I hated it when he did this—he enjoyed peeking into my mind and saying random things when I least expected it. "You were reading my mind just now, weren't you?"

He shook his head. "No, I just have been around you long enough to know what you are thinking. I hate it."

He had a point, I knew them pretty well too, whether I wanted to or not. They weren't that horrible, especially compared to other gods we had run into, such as Demeter. They also were better company than any other friend I had as a human, as they all wanted to use me. I guess it was just hard for me to get used to, as I didn't have anyone who I stayed with not want to kick me out, other than Chrys.

Prometheus was the only one I wasn't sure about. When this all started, he was terrified of Zeus, but now he would stand up right before him and lie about being married to Chrys. Not only that, but now he had to spend some time each year in the Underworld with Chrys. That just made little sense. Who would do that for someone they didn't know all that well? I mean, I would do it for Chrys without a doubt, but he didn't have the relationship that we did. Not to mention all these gods hated the Underworld.

Something was off, I could feel it.

"Do you trust Prometheus?" I asked the others. I had asked this question multiple times, but I still wasn't sure what they really thought. They had said they did, but I wanted to know what they thought.

"I do," Mel said.

I rolled my eyes. That made sense. "Well, of course you do, you are infatuated with him. But Pothos, what do you think?"

Pothos paused and then shrugged. "I think he has his own motives, yes, but I don't think it'll be outright betrayal like you are thinking. I think he just hates Zeus and wants to see him suffer."

"Stopping this wedding won't make him suffer though, it will just stop the wedding and help Chrys. I doubt Zeus cares about marrying her."

"I suppose. But Chrys has the power to bring down Zeus. He is probably hoping if he sides with her, she will eventually end him."

He had a point. Being so close to her, he could convince her to take him down. But was that what we wanted? Would Chrys even win, let alone want to perform such a task?

I asked, "She was part of a prophecy, right? That the daughter of Hades would bring down Olympus and it would bring a new era of the gods."

He nodded. "Yup, which is why Zeus cursed Hades to never be able to have kids, although apparently he wasn't successful with that."

Every time I heard that part of the story, it made me sick. Sure, I didn't want kids, but to take away that choice for someone else was disgusting, not to mention inhumane. "I presume Hades didn't have a say in that?"

"No, he didn't. Zeus isn't one to ask permissions. Most of the shit he does is because he wants to, not because he thinks it's for the greater good. I mean, if the prophecy is true, and us, quote unquote, lesser gods become the new reigning leaders, it would mean that she will destroy Poseidon, Hades, Demeter, Persephone as well. Just like the titans were all those years ago."

"Except for Prometheus?"

Pothos nodded. "Yeah, and a couple of others could save their skin. That's what happens when you are a kiss-ass to the strongest existing."

I forgot that Prometheus isn't a god, but a titan. I still didn't quite understand what the difference was, just that one is an older god. Somehow survived, mainly by making Zeus happy, or entertaining him as I knew he had been tortured a few times by Zeus. "So that is pretty much what Prometheus is doing now, being a kiss ass to whom he believes is the strongest existing?"

"Seems like it."

I guess that made sense. After being alive for so long, you figured out how to stay alive. "I don't think Chrys would ever purposefully take out her father and all the others though. Maybe just Poseidon and Zeus."

"Yeah, I couldn't see it either, but from what I know about the gods in Olympus, you just never know."

I shook my head. "No, she would never hurt her father. She loves him too much. She would do anything for him."

"Including marrying Zeus, I suppose. I mean, that was why she did it, right? To save her father's life?"

I thought back at that fight in London almost a year before. Zeus was about to kill Hades right in front of her when she made the proposal. I didn't think she would ever do such a thing, but she cared enough to save her father's life, to sacrifice herself. That was why her father and I went to such lengths to save her. She was pure-hearted. "Yeah, I suppose it was."

We were all quiet for a moment, recalling that day. So much had happened since then, not to mention the others were confronting Zeus at the moment. This was the key moment.

What if it just broke out in a fight just like that night?

I shook my head. "That night was horrifying."

Pothos nodded. "Yes, it was. Other than Poseidon

taking on Chrys. That shit was hilarious."

A.J. mumbled something under the tape. We all glanced over at him. He kept making noise. He was getting on my nerves again.

"What is it A.J.? Hard to speak under that tape?" Pothos asked.

"Should we take it off? I'm a little curious if I need to punch him for his comments or not."

Pothos shrugged. "Sure, we can always put it back on if need be."

I got up and pulled it off of him. He took a deep breath and smiled.

"So you think that was funny? Being killed and reanimated again and again?" He asked.

That was a weird comment. "Yeah, it was. Poseidon had it coming for trying to kidnap her. Just like you have Tartarus waiting for you when Hades comes back."

"You know, you all aren't as smart as I thought. A.J. had said for the longest time that you would be so hard to convince, especially after going through everything you had gone through."

Pothos stood up. "Shit, Huntley get back!"

I jumped back as a figure seemed to leap out of A.J.'s body. A.J.'s head dropped and suddenly in front of him was another person.

"Fuck," I whispered as I stared at Poseidon. He had us all fooled—somehow he was able to stay inside the body of his son. Poseidon was just using him to get information he needed and was just planning to escape at the right moment.

And that was at this moment.

"Thank you so much for all your information, especially about the wedding between Prometheus and Chrys being fake, and how she is married to a mere human. I'm sure Zeus will reward me dearly for this information."

I shook my head. "No, you said…"

"I said what? Oh, that I would attack after she was leaving. I'm not stupid, not after last time. I know I am no match for her. Zeus is though, especially since she doesn't know how to use her powers on command. But I am also thankful for the information about Prometheus and how he would betray Zeus by training her. I can finally get rid of that traitor once and for all."

Mel threw a black strand of lightning at Poseidon, but it did nothing. He was a lot stronger than her. He was stronger than any of us.

He laughed. "There is no use trying to stop me! You are all weaklings! But I don't want to get rid of you just yet. I want so much payback for what you have put me through in the last couple of days, starting with you Huntley."

He snapped his fingers, and we were suddenly tied to chairs.

I shook my head. "No, you can't do this. Zeus will kill her!"

Poseidon acted like he was thinking for a moment. "Oh really? I didn't realize that. That's the point, human! Someone like her shouldn't exist. She can destroy all of Olympus if she wanted, and when you have been granted immortality, having a threat of something that will take that away is a little terrifying. Death is not something we face openly like you humans. You do not understand what the meaning of death is to us."

"But you will kill someone innocent?"

"Kill or be dead. That is what it is like to live as a god. Now." He snapped his fingers again and tape appeared over my mouth. "I want you to remember that you could not, in fact, save your precious Chrys because of your stupidity. You let me in your home, you made sure A.J. came with you, and you were stupid enough to think some rope would keep me down." He laughed. "Now, I have to go stop a fake wedding from being granted by Zeus."

We watched as he left the apartment. Tears

blurred my eyes. No, this wasn't happening. This couldn't be real.

I had to save Chrys.

Luckily, I was a punk and if you could know one thing about punks, it was that we always had a pocket knife up our sleeves. I just had to figure out how to get it out and get us out of here. And quick.

Chapter 25

CHRYS

I trembled, even after eating three seeds, as we made our way up to Zeus' palace. My father placed his hand on my shoulder, as if he noticed my worry. I felt a lot better now that he was here. He always kept me safe, and I knew his plan would be a success. He was the smartest of all the gods, mainly because he kept to himself. None of the other gods had a reason to have a problem with my father. They just found him odd.

Prometheus didn't seem worried, and honestly, he should be the most worried. If this all went south, Zeus would take out most of his anger on him. He had faced Zeus' wrath before—if I were him I don't think I could go through with crossing him again.

I guess I was in the same boat though.

If Zeus figured out I was lying, he will kill me right then and there. I didn't know if that was worse than marrying him, but I didn't want my father to deal with me being gone. Or, I guess, sent to Tartarus. After my recent interaction with the place, I didn't want to go back. Yet, Zeus had the power to lock gods away in that dungeon.

Fun fun.

But now that father was here, the likelihood of Zeus killing me was much less. Father would come up with some other plan that would push back the inevitable. Or, at least, I hoped.

I wondered about Prometheus still, though. He had gone off with Apollo, which didn't seem like a good thing. What if all of this was a ruse and he would turn me in to Zeus for some reward?

No, that made little sense—he would have said something to Zeus earlier. Waiting all this time would just put himself more in jeopardy, not earning him more of a reward. No, he was definitely on our side to take Zeus down, but I couldn't help but feel he had an ulterior motive.

As for Apollo, I didn't know what could be going through his mind. I didn't trust him at all and did not like that he talked to Prometheus without us hearing what he had to say. Maybe they had history, yes, but so far, any history that anyone has had in Olympus was not helpful as I had discovered. They all had a lot of baggage.

Different gods and goddesses seemed to give us looks as we made our way through the city. I didn't know if it was because they saw me, or Hades, or Prometheus. It was probably all of us, as I had never been in Olympus. Father was usually never here, and I had no idea for Prometheus. He was a titan, which I figured meant that he didn't get much support from most of the gods. Zeus had killed most of his kind and put them down in Tartarus.

So, I understood why he wanted to screw over Zeus.

We made it up to the palace and two centurion guards opened the giant gold doors that led into the palace. We didn't even have to say anything or show anything. I wondered if it was because father was there, and he was the brother of Zeus. He was one of the big three, so to speak.

It would be a lie to say I was surprised to find Zeus on a chaise being fed grapes by beautiful nymphs. It was the most stereotypical thing I had ever seen, more stereotypical than my father wearing black all the time.

Meh, it was about even.

He smiled brightly, to my disgust. "My bride-to-be, what brings you up here, and with your mother and father and…" he then noticed Prometheus with us. His eyes turned dark. "Ladies, please leave us."

The nymphs did as ordered and left us to talk. I picked at my nails, worry engulfing me. Zeus got up from his chair and stood straight.

"I have a feeling I will not like what you all have to say, brother."

Father stood tall and didn't budge. "This wedding cannot go on."

Zeus raised an eyebrow. "Oh, and why is that?"

"She and I have been married according to the marriage laws of the Underworld," Prometheus explained, wavering a little, which was probably because of the seeds.

Zeus laughed and scratched the scruff on his face. "Oh really? You are going to cross me like this, Prometheus? I didn't even know you knew each other."

Prometheus wrapped his arm around me, his hand going a little too low for comfort, but I didn't let that show. "She and I met while she was in London. We hit it off and are in love. Using the pomegranate seeds, we have wed."

"Fell in love, eh? Why did you think it was a good idea to marry when the reason for our marriage is so I can monitor her and her powers?" Zeus sat back down and took a deep breath. "I mean, that was the deal so I don't kill her."

"Prometheus can look after her in the Underworld, and I'll keep watch the rest of the time."

Zeus let out a chuckle. "No offense, but I don't trust either of you. You, brother, especially. You went against my command for having a child."

Father frowned. "You and I know that it wasn't planned."

I didn't know how I felt about the way father said that, but I understood. I wasn't supposed to be born yet here I was, alive and kicking. But hearing how he didn't want me in the beginning was a little hurtful.

"There is still the fact that I don't trust Prometheus. It wouldn't be the first time he has undermined me."

Prometheus held me even tighter. "This time is different, this time it has to do with love."

Zeus rolled his eyes. "Love. Right."

"It's not a lie," I totally lied. I grabbed Prometheus' hand. "We love each other and want to be with each other. We took the pomegranate seeds to do just that. It wasn't like I would be monitored at all the time here anyway, and Prometheus could just watch over me in the Underworld. Hell, you could just send Hermes down. He did a good job watching me. You trust him, right?"

Zeus seemed to ponder on this, as if I had made a decent point. Hermes had served him for a long time, and I wouldn't mind if he was in the Underworld. My father, on the other hand, will probably stab him after a few decades.

Zeus took a deep breath. "You know, you make an excellent point but I just don't think you two love each other, which makes me suspicious."

"We love each other," Prometheus said as he pulled me in for a kiss. "See?"

Prometheus kissed me, hard. I wanted to be taken aback, push him away, but between the fact I had to make it look like the two of us were an item, and the fact I was still on those pomegranate seeds, I made it pretty convincing. My body felt as if it was melting in his arms as I wrapped my arms around him to draw him closer. He ran his fingers through my hair, as my hand made it down his back and into his back pockets.

What the hell was wrong with me?

I enjoyed the taste—his mouth tasted like cinnamon and nutmeg, almost like a chai tea. I wondered what more he was capable of.

No, I loved Huntley. But I had to admit, something about Prometheus was rather sexy.

"That's enough," my father interrupted and Prometheus pulled his head back, but kept his arms around me.

"Proof enough?" Prometheus asked.

"It was definitely entertaining, but I don't know if I would say it was proof. I mean, for starters, why didn't my precious Flower ever tell me she was in love with another man? This all could have been stopped earlier if she just had said something."

I shook my head, and ignored the sickening feeling I had when he called me his Flower. I saw Father tense as well.

"Because you wouldn't have listened to me. If I told you I loved someone else, would you have said okay or would you have killed them outright and said you were done with it?"

Zeus smiled. "So instead, you waited until mommy and daddy were here to protect you?"

I didn't respond since, well, that kind of is what happened.

"Or I guess it was more so you could do the ceremony. Right before ours. A little bit of a dick move, to be honest."

"A dick move for a dick god," Hades commented. I couldn't believe he said that. I guess he liked to bicker with most of the gods.

Zeus stood back up. "The point still stands; the marriage was in exchange for your life. I feel since you broke your part of the bargain, that I should be able to take back mine."

"It isn't a fair bargain and you know it, Zeus." Hades growled. "This is a way that we all win, and you can have Hermes watch over her in the Underworld, or have random visits with him. He knows how to sneak into the Underworld in ways I haven't even been able to figure out."

Zeus seemed to ponder this. "Give me a few days to figure out what I want to do. I'm not guaranteeing It won't end here, but I will think about the option you have presented."

I couldn't believe what I was hearing. He would let me stay in the Underworld with Prometheus… With father… With Huntley.

Suddenly the doors to the palace opened, and a figure came running in.

"What is the meaning of this?" Zeus proclaimed.

"Oh, Poseidon, what is it?"

Shit.

"They are lying to you!" Poseidon exclaimed. "She is not married to Prometheus, but that human Huntley. They have been scheming this entire time on how to dethrone you from Olympus!"

Chapter 26

HUNTLEY

Shit, now what were we going to do?

I glanced over at Pothos and Mel who were both tied up as well as I was. A.J. was still passed out, but I would definitely be beating him up later.

I could hardly move anything. Normally when someone tied me up, I had ways to make it so my wrists or hands weren't as tight—something you learned while being a delinquent. However, since Poseidon used his powers, I wasn't able to do that. Maneuvering to get my knife had become a great hassle that I didn't think was possible at this point.

The other problem was that I was gagged. Otherwise, I could tell Pothos and Mel that I had a knife that they could try to grab.

Oh wait, they enjoyed reading my mind.

I wobbled in my chair to catch their attention. They glanced over to me and I just prayed that they would figure out what I wanted.

Read my mind, god damn it.

Pothos hopped over to me on his chair. He did it, yes. Or at least, he figured it out. Pothos mentioned that it isn't like reading minds directly, but more of an understanding of the emotion that was going on. Ironically, it was both Pothos and Mel that could read minds, and few other gods could do the same. Pothos could do it because he understood passion and Mel because she could create nightmares.

Sleeping in the same flat as them had been an adventure.

The next part would be awkward as I needed to get in a position allowing Pothos the ability to maneuver his fingers up my sleeve and grab my knife. I had learned over the years keeping the knife up my sleeve was a lot easier to deal with than having one in a pocket. With the right movement of the arm, you could get it into your arm and didn't need to reach down to your pocket, which made other thugs and punks realize what you were doing.

Yeah, my childhood was messed up.

I was able to move to a position where Pothos

could reach up my sleeve of my hoodie. He maneuvered a bit until he grasped hold of it. I heard a metallic sound hit the tile floor.

Well, at least it was out of my sleeve.

I moved back and forth until I could slowly get the chair to fall to the ground with me in it. I scooted across the floor until I felt the metal in my hand. With a flick of my thumb, I heard it open.

And that was how it was done.

I flipped the knife around so I could saw at my own ropes. I just hoped a normal human knife could get through these ropes. Knowing this world, probably not. I felt the rope give a little, which meant it did.

Thank goodness he used regular ropes.

A couple of moments passed, and I had cut the rope all the way through. I was able to bring my arms forward and took the cloth out of my mouth.

"Oh thank god that worked, otherwise we would be fucked."

I cut through the rope that tied my legs when there was a knock at the door. All of us froze.

"Persephone, it's me Hermes!"

I debated on what I should do. He helped us before, but did that mean we could trust him? I moved the cloth from Pothos mouth.

"Let him in."

I hurried over to the door and opened it. Hermes stepped in and saw Pothos and Mel tied up.

"Huh. Didn't think you two were still a couple. Kinky."

"No, you dimwit," Pothos said. "Poseidon possessed A.J. and is now going to Zeus to tell him what is going on and how Prometheus and Chrys are not actually married."

Hermes hurried over to untie Mel. "Well don't just sit there, we better go before he gets to Zeus!"

I had a feeling we were too late to beat him, but we could at least save Chrys from Zeus. I helped Pothos get untied, and we hurried out the door towards the Temple.

"Wait, is it okay if Huntley is out in public? Humans aren't allowed in Olympus," Pothos said.

Hermes looked back at me. "I think at this point it will be fine. There are many more reasons for Zeus to kill him compared to this latest so-called breach of rules."

I had to admit, he had a point. There were many reasons for Zeus to kill me compared to just being caught up here. If he knew that Chrys, and I were married, he probably would turn me into a fly and squash me. Just like his wife tried to do.

Man, I loved being human.

Olympus was like a big maze. I wondered how gods could make their way through this all. Could Chrys do it? Did she understand all this chaos? Although Hades' castle took a while to figure out, it wasn't as crazy as this. It only took me a few weeks to figure out the layout of the areas Hades said I could be in, and then some.

I was so glad he never caught me.

Hades was with Chrys right now, which made me feel a little better. As long as he was next to her, he wouldn't let Zeus or Poseidon harm Chrys. I wasn't sure what I could do to help her at this moment, as I had no power over Poseidon or Zeus. They were both a lot stronger than me. I mean, a whole lot stronger. But with the others here, I could figure out something. Maybe they could distract the gods while I ran off with Chrys. Yeah, that sounded like a plausible plan.

As we rounded a corner, closer to the palace now, a man in sunglasses held up his hands. "Woah there, where's the rush?"

"Apollo," Hermes growled. "What are you doing here?"

So this was Apollo. Yeah, he looked like a douche. I could see why Chrys didn't like him. He put his hands in his pockets and shrugged. "Out and about, watching the sun to make sure light touches everything that is needed. Just as I do every day."

"Well, if you don't mind, we are in quite a bit of a hurry."

"Going to go stop Poseidon, I presume?"

Shit, what did he know?

"Get out of our way right now, if you know what is good for you."

Apollo let out a little laugh. "Oh Hermes, you would not win against me. Now, how about the four of you just cool it for a moment and realize you can't save Chrys."

"So, you're siding with Zeus?" Pothos asked. "I don't understand why—you hate him."

"I never said I was helping Zeus. There is a lot more going on than you realize."

Mel stepped forward. "Move it or I will make you relive all the losses you have experienced, Apollo. And yes, I know about all of them."

His lips curled. "Always so fast to resort to torture. No wonder Prometheus keeps you around, he is definitely the masochist." Apollo stepped forward and caressed her cheek. "And believe me, I would know. Especially after what he and I did last night."

Mel looked like she was about to murder someone. "You fucking dog, you knew he was mine!"

"Yes, but he and I had a little… business to discuss. Then one thing led to another, just as it always does."

"Which was what?" Pothos asked.

Apollo glanced over at the palace. "Oh, you all will see soon. Nevertheless, I can't have you go to Zeus' palace just yet."

I did not like where this was headed. If he wasn't with Zeus, then why couldn't we go? What was going on? What did he and Prometheus discuss last night?

What did he want with Chrys?

"We have to stop Poseidon, he will try to get Zeus to kill Chrys," I said.

He patted me on the head. "Oh, the human speaks. What do you think you will do to stop Poseidon, hmm? Use your… knife? Or… I don't even know, what are humans capable of?"

I just glared at him. He had a point, and I really hated that.

"Prometheus was going to act like he is married to Chrys. If he knew that would fail this entire time, then what are you two planning? And how do you believe it will…" Pothos gasped. "No, he wouldn't."

Apollo said nothing, but grinned.

A loud explosion erupted from the palace.

"Ah, that is my cue. It has been great, gents, my lady. I have a feeling our paths will cross again."

With that, he turned into a wolf and ran off as fast as he could towards the entrance of the palace. So that was what Chrys meant when she said beware of wolves.

"What is he doing?" I asked Pothos.

He shook his head. "No time to explain, we have to hurry! Hermes, can you fly ahead and help Chrys? We will be right behind."

Hermes nodded and took off towards the palace after Apollo. He was a lot faster than I even realized. But at least he was on our side.

Pothos started running, and Mel and I followed. I just prayed with everything that was going on, that Chrys would be okay.

Chapter 27

CHRYS

"Don't you dare touch my daughter!" Hades held up his hand as the blackness of death swirled above his hand. I could feel it radiating through the room —the familiar feeling of death soothing me even with all the chaos that was going on all around me. My father's power was familiar and even though it had only been a few days, it felt nice.

Poseidon raised his own arm and a ball of water and earth started to form. The rocks swirled with a couple of gallons of water, sloshing in a sphere. He threw it straight at father. Father deflected it with his own sphere.

"Do that again and I will take you down, Poseidon."

"It isn't Poseidon that you should worry about, Hades," Zeus interrupted. Zeus almost appeared taller than before, and larger, as if he could be any more intimidating. "I am the one who will kill your daughter."

Father turned to him, snarling. I have seen my father angry before, but never this angry. "Don't make me do this, brother. I will not let you touch her."

Zeus shot a piece of lightning next to my father, who didn't even flinch. "It is your fault that things ended this way. If you didn't fool me like you did, then this wouldn't be a problem. Your daughter would be safe."

Black tendrils stretched out of my father's arms, thrashing every which way. Zeus didn't even move as he struck next to him. Hades yelled. "Yeah, like all the other women in your life were safe. I don't believe for a second that you intended to help her— you just want to fuck everyone."

Zeus let out a laugh as he held his hand, lightning forming. "Oh, you know me too well. But that doesn't change the fact that your daughter should not exist. Say goodbye to her, this is the last you will ever see of her."

I took a step back. This would not end well. I

didn't know what I would do as I watched the three gods size each other up, as if this would be a fight with only one of them coming out alive.

I knew I had to do something.

"Over my dead body." The darkness around my father got bigger.

Zeus shrugged. "If I must."

"Wait!" Prometheus shouted. "No one needs to die, just hear us out!"

Zeus turned to him and yelled. "Enough out of you! You will be dealt with shortly. You think generations of an eagle eating out your liver every day was bad, just wait to see what I have in store for you."

Prometheus backed up like he would run, but stayed put. Honestly, if I were him, I would have run. There wasn't anything he could do in this situation, not with these three gods. They were the strongest out of all of them. But he stayed where he was, just a few feet from me.

My mother hurried over to me and wrapped her arms around me. I didn't know what to do with her around me like this—I wasn't used to her embracing me like this, and in this case, it was like she wanted to keep me safe, but I knew she couldn't stop anything. She would only be killed right before me.

I couldn't let her do that. I had to protect her—to protect all of them. Huntley was in Olympus as well, and if this went down horribly, Zeus would kill him.

No, nothing would help right now.

Zeus held up his arms and lightning exploded in the room, the windows exploding glass everywhere. Glass cut up my mother and I's arms. That would hurt later when I washed it out, especially the little shards that were embedded in the cuts.

This was it, this was the end.

Father parried the attack, and darkness exploded in the room. It differed from the darkness that surrounded me. Mine felt raw and wild, but his was more controlled and precise. I wished I could do that, but I wasn't skilled enough yet to control my powers like him. Right now, I really wished I could, as I would be able to help him without losing control and hurting everyone.

No, I had to help. If this was a fight, I might as well try to stop everything.

I could feel the darkness engulf me as energy from Zeus, Hades, and Poseidon erupted. There was so much power in this room, I wondered if the palace would even survive. I felt the power of sea and earth hit me, but I blocked with my power of death. I struck it straight at Poseidon, hoping it would knock him down again. He could block it this time.

I wish I had killed him the last time we had fought, or at least kept him dead.

"So, she shows her true colors. This is exactly what I feared," Zeus said as a bolt of lightning formed in his hand. "Now, she must be destroyed."

Father threw a ball of dark energy at Zeus. Zeus deflected, and it crashed into a beam, making pieces of the ceiling come down on us.

"How dare you keep defying me brother!" Zeus yelled at him, his voice loud enough to feel it in my bones. It was terrifying to say the least. I wished I could just run away, but I had a feeling I wouldn't even make it out of this room if I turned my back to either of the gods.

Father yelled back. "How dare you keep trying to kill my one and only daughter!"

Poseidon interjected. "Just get on with it! You are doing more talking than killing!"

"Shut up, like you have been doing anything other than trying to get killed." Zeus formed another lightning bolt. "Just don't get killed this time, okay."

I formed more darkness and death with my own

hands. "I'm not afraid of you, Zeus, I will take you down even if it means my own death."

"Wait!" Hermes came running into the palace. Everything seemed to stop for a moment, none of us expecting someone to enter while all this power was erupting. I mean, I sure as hell didn't.

Hermes bent forwards, as if he was out of breath from running up here. "You all just need to stop!"

Zeus stepped forward to him, his lips curled in an ironic smile. "Ah, Hermes. Don't worry, I have a bone to pick with you later. I am very curious how all of this could go down when you were the one in charge of it all."

Hermes stood tall, as if proclaiming to Zeus that he wasn't afraid of him. "Zeus, for once in your life, talk something out! She doesn't deserve to die!"

Zeus turned to look at me. I froze in my spot, my power still at my fingertips, waiting to be used. "I see, so you grew a soft spot for her. Here I thought your hatred for Hades would make it so you wouldn't betray me. I guess I was wrong."

"Just listen!"

Zeus did just the opposite and threw another lightning bolt at me. I grabbed my mother and jumped out of the way and sent a blast towards him. He reflected it. He was not as easy as Poseidon to hit. I was not strong enough to stop this, and I was running out of time.

Stepping forward towards me, Zeus began shouting at me. "Just give in, Chrys, you cannot take me down. Even your own father can't take me down."

"You haven't seen what I am actually capable of, brother. I might surprise you." Father sent another flash of darkness at him. He hit it straight on and fell. He was still moving though, as it didn't knock him completely out. Poseidon took the chance to knock Hades to the ground with a blow of water.

This was a complete disaster. I didn't know what I should do. I was not strong enough to defeat Zeus. I glanced over at Prometheus, who still stood there, either in shock or knowing there was no way Zeus would let him out of this room alive. I crouched down as an enormous piece of rock hit the wall above my head and hurried over to Prometheus. "What do we do?"

He shook his head. "I have no idea. I guess, when the right distraction happens, we should get out of here."

"No, I can't leave my father behind."

"You will die otherwise."

"I can't run away. It isn't like me."

Prometheus' shoulders and face slumped in defeat. "I guess this will be harder than I had hoped."

This was always harder than I hoped. I just wanted to see what the mortal realm was like, but I had to get into this piece of shit situation. This past year was anything but easy. But I couldn't rely on anyone anymore. I had to find my way out of this. I had to use all my powers to get out of this alive.

I just hoped no one I cared about would get hurt in the process.

"Usually is. Well, I guess I should fight." I ran forward and shot another black bolt towards Poseidon. He blocked it, then sent a sphere of water and earth at me. It hit me full force. I felt like I was drowning, unable to breathe. I panicked, things feeling like they were crushing me and grabbing me. It reminded me of when he took me under the water in London, when everything was suffocating me and I did not know what would happen. I didn't know what would happen now. Was he going to kill me? Was he going to take me to his lair? Everything was spiraling out of control again and I didn't know what to do.

Energy shot out of me in every direction like tentacles of death. The strongest was aimed straight at Poseidon, just like that day. I wanted him dead—I wanted him out of my life. He caused the problem the first time on earth, and it was his son that betrayed me. This was all Poseidon's fault.

Poseidon was suddenly lifted up by the tentacles, his body seizing in pain. This time I would not bring him back to life, this time I would make sure he stayed dead.

With all my power, I shot him out the window.

Was he dead? Or did I just stun him like last time?

I calmed myself down. The black tendrils disappeared as everything came back to me. I had been fighting Poseidon, and this was what happened—I lost control of who I was yet again.

I was the monster that Zeus made me out to be.

"Poseidon!" Zeus jumped out the window after him. For a moment, it was silent.

Hades hurried over to me. "Let's get out of here. We can hide in the Underworld, he can't come down there."

He grabbed my arm, and we started for the entry. I didn't protest as I didn't know how to respond—I didn't know how I would get out of this without my father's help. I just hoped that I could stay alive long enough to see Huntley again.

As we almost made it out, a figure stopped us. I

looked up to see a familiar face—the same face I had to stay in an apartment next to. It was Apollo.

Father yelled at him. "Get out of the way, Apollo, or I swear I will send you to Tartarus."

"Sorry, Hades. I can't."

"And why not?" Hades growled.

He nodded towards Prometheus. "I promised him I would do this." He held up his hand and snapped his fingers.

Everything went black, including the sky.

It was like someone had turned off the sun. Apollo had turned off the sun. But why?

I felt someone put their arm around me and a piece of glass go over my mouth. I pushed and shoved whoever it was, but I could feel the liquid going down my throat. I was beginning to feel so dizzy and lightheaded. The last things I remembered was father yelling and streaks of lightning going through the sky.

Chapter 28

HUNTLEY

What the hell was that?

Everything had just gone dark and now lightning was exploding in the sky. Holy shit, what was going on up there?

We still ran, carefully now that the lights were out except for the light coming from the lightning. I just hoped Chrys was okay.

"This can't be good," Pothos yelled. "The only reason all light would be out like this is if Apollo did something."

What did that mean? What were Apollo and Prometheus up to? And what did they want with Chrys? Were they going to hurt her?

"How could he do that?"

Pothos sighed. "He is the god of light. He has the power to turn it off any time he wants. I knew he would do something, but I didn't think it would be something like this. There will be hell to pay if Zeus catches him."

It seemed like Pothos had figured out what was going on, but he hadn't told us what it was. He could trick both Mel and Pothos and not have them suspect a thing. I always figured he was up to something, but trusted him because of these two. Apparently, my suspicion was spot on.

At least I could trust these two. And probably Hermes.

We reached the top of the hill where the palace was. Olympus was still in darkness, other than the bolts of lightning. Zeus must have been freaking out about the sun going out, because I know I sure was.

Was the sun out on Earth? How was this even physically possible? Did he just hide it? Was this like a solar eclipse? I never got to see one when I was alive, so although it was kind of cool to see how darkness could just suddenly fall, it was also scary how everything went quiet.

As we entered the palace, everything lit up again. I found Hades and Persephone there, Hades was angry and freaking out. Persephone was crying as

Hermes held her. Zeus was yelling at some people.

"What the hell…" I whispered.

Zeus pointed at us. "You! Where did you all take her?"

Hades shook his head. "They did not take her or else they wouldn't be here!"

Zeus walked up to me and grabbed me by the collar. "Do you have any idea how much trouble you are in for being here? Do any of you know how much trouble you are all in?!"

"You mean we all stood up for what we thought was right?" Mel questioned.

Zeus turned to her, throwing me to the side. "Oh yeah? Well now Poseidon almost died, and your lovely Chrys has been kidnapped by Prometheus and Apollo. If I had a guess, they are taking her somewhere to brainwash her into trying to kill us all."

Poseidon was almost killed? More importantly, Chrys was kidnapped?

"Prometheus used the vial of Lethe," Pothos said. "I got that when I read Apollo's desires."

"It doesn't change the fact that Chrys almost killed Poseidon yet again!" Zeus yelled. "And it is because of all of you!" He held up his arm and lightning formed in his hand.

"They didn't know Prometheus would do this!" Hades exclaimed. "If you just let her stay in the Underworld, none of this would have happened!"

Oh no, another god fight. Is this all they did because stories seemed to be pointed in that direction?

"And if you just let me marry her, then I wouldn't have to kill her!"

Zeus threw the lightning at Hades. Hades blocked it and threw a ball of darkness at him. Persephone was still crying, and Hermes looked as if he didn't know what he would do next. He was in this shit as deep as we were.

"Everyone just stop it for a second!" Persephone yelled. "Let's just discuss this like civilized people, is that so hard?!"

Zeus and Hades slowly lowered their arms, but still glared at each other.

Persephone went on. "Now, we need to figure out what to do to find Chrys. If Prometheus gave her the vial, then she is in grave danger! He will convince her that they are helping her and how to use her powers against us."

"Which is exactly what I was afraid of all this time."

"If you just let her stay in the Underworld, then

none of this would have happened!" Hades shot back.

"This arguing isn't helping get Chrys back!" I exclaimed, sick of their bickering. I couldn't even take in everything that had happened yet. Could she really be taken just like that? There was no way Prometheus was strong enough to take Chrys. Pothos was right, they must have used that vial so she would pass out just like Hera did. And if that was the case, how much did he use? What would she forget?

He had been excited when I brought that vial back. Did he have this planned the entire time? Was he wanting to use it specifically on her?

"You all will not be doing anything," Zeus said. "You all will be under arrest while my people look for her."

Hades shook his head. "No, she is my daughter. I will look for her until it kills me."

"Which it just might, brother. Did it occur to you that Prometheus might use her to kill you as well?"

"She wouldn't hurt me." Hades said. I agreed, she wouldn't hurt him, even if she forgot who he was. I felt like deep down, she would always remember her father. They were too close to ever hurt each other. At least, I hope that was the case.

"She wouldn't? What if she didn't remember you? What if she thought you were the enemy because she may have been wiped of her memories by Prometheus and Apollo? Did that occur to you? That she might be transformed into someone unstoppable?"

All of us were quiet. If Chrys really forgot her father, that meant she would have also forgotten me. Would she ever be able to remember? Would there be any possible way?

Hades was the first to speak. "No, she is stronger than Lethe. I believe she will recall her memories as long as she can hold onto something she loves." Hades glanced over at me but said nothing. I knew what I needed to do.

"Whatever you say, brother, but that doesn't mean I will forgive her for almost killing Poseidon. Had she succeeded, she could take out the two of us as well."

"But she won't hurt me. I will get her to remember and then take her down to the Underworld where you will never hear a peep from us ever again."

Zeus scratched the scruff on his face. "How about this, dear brother, whoever finds her first will decide her fate. If you can get her to the Underworld, then so be it. I won't come after you. But if I find her when you do, it is the battle to end all battles."

"Fine, brother," Hades held out his hand. "It's a deal."

Thank You For Reading!

Thank you so much for reading! Readers like you make it possible for authors like me to write stories! If you could spare a moment and leave a review on Amazon, Goodreads, BookBub, and wherever you like to buy books, that would mean the world to me! It really helps authors like me to succeed in the publishing world.

A big thank you again for your patronage. I hope you will check out the next book in the series and my other series. Book 4: Enchanted will be available November 2020!

Acknowledgments

I want to thank everyone who made this novel possible. A big thank you to my editor Justin Boyer who hopefully hasn't gotten sick of reading my stories yet. Thank you to Biserka Design for the amazing covers for this series! I love them lot! A special thank you to Dr. Almira Poudrier at ASU for answering my questions about Greek Mythology as things get weird and confusing and even more weird. And, lastly, thank you to my husband and parents who are always supporting me.

About the Author

Dani Hoots is a science fiction, fantasy, romance, and young adult author who loves anything with a story. She has a B.S. in Anthropology, a Masters of Urban and Environmental Planning, a Certificate in Novel Writing from Arizona State University, and a BS in Herbal Science from Bastyr University.

Currently she is working on a YA urban fantasy series called Daughter of Hades, a YA urban fantasy series called The Wonderland Chronicles, a historic fantasy vampire series called A World of Vampires, and a YA sci-fi series called Sanshlian Series. She has also started up an indie publishing company called FoxTales Press. She also works with Anthill Studios in creating comics through Antik Comics.

Her hobbies include reading, watching anime, cooking, studying different languages, wire walking, hula hoop, and working with plants. She is also an herbalist and sells her concoctions on FoxCraft Apothecary. She lives in Phoenix with her husband and visits Seattle often.

Feel free to email her with any questions you might have!
danihootsauthor@gmail.com